"I mu...
Such a g........

Raoul put a finger under her chin and wrenched her face up toward him. Then, with a contemptuous gesture, he turned away.

How ironic, Jenni thought. If only during the past week someone had added a surname to the title Monsieur Raoul, a horrified realization would have come and she could have fled, her cloak of anonymity secure. She sprang to her feet. "I shall leave Les Forêts tomorrow."

"Determined to play the part to the end, eh?" Raoul's voice was sarcastic. "I shall inform our lawyer. You came in secret to give Les Forêts the once-over, didn't you—to see whether your inheritance would be worth claiming—"

"My inheritance?" Jenni gaped at him in stupefaction.

Rachel Ford was born in Coventry, descended from a long line of Warwickshire farmers. She met her husband at Birmingham University, and he is now a principal lecturer in a polytechnic school. Rachel and her husband both taught school in the West Indies for several years after their marriage and have had fabulous holidays in Mexico, Venezuela and Ecuador during revolutions and coups! Their two daughters were born in England. After stints as a teacher and information guide, Rachel took up writing, which she really enjoys doing the most—first children's and girls' stories, and finally Romance novels.

Books by Rachel Ford

HARLEQUIN ROMANCE
2913—CLOUDED PARADISE
  21—BRING BACK YESTERDAY

Heirs
to Loving
Rachel Ford

Harlequin Books

TORONTO • NEW YORK • LONDON
AMSTERDAM • PARIS • SYDNEY • HAMBURG
STOCKHOLM • ATHENS • TOKYO • MILAN

Original hardcover edition published in 1988
by Mills & Boon Limited

ISBN 0-373-17038-6

Harlequin Romance first edition May 1989

CHAPTER ONE

THERE was no warning of the car's approach. It roared round the corner, far too fast, as Jenni continued her grim struggle with the punctured wheel. The driver jammed on his—she felt instinctively that it *was* a he—his brakes and scorched to a reluctant halt, from the sound of it, barely an inch from her bumper.

There was silence for a moment, except for the rattle of little pebbles settling back on to the surface of the lane, then a long, imperious blast on a horn, which made her start, almost swallowing the nut she was holding between her teeth. She turned sharply, but all she could see from her position, crouched at the back of the van, was a large, aggressive-looking headlamp. There was another strident blast on the horn and Jenni flapped her hand angrily.

'Oh, just go away, will you?' What was the matter with the man? Couldn't he see that she was in trouble?

A car door slammed loudly, making her jump again, then footsteps crunched over the gravel so that, in spite of herself, a frisson of unease ran through her.

'*Qu'est ce que vous faites? Vous êtes idiote, ou quoi?*'

Jenni's head jerked round at the fury in the man's voice. He was standing right at her shoulder, so that she saw first a pair of black leather shoes, then her eyes travelled—a long way—up a pair of light-grey-suited legs, up past a formidable chest and shoulders, confined within a pristine white shirt and pale grey jacket to——

The nut dropped from her open mouth and tinkled away

5

unheeded as, with a silent groan of anguish, she stared up at the man, aghast. Well, well, she thought involuntarily, as she slowly straightened up to face him, some Gallic fate was having quite a field day with her: a mugging, a puncture and—and once more, for the second time that day, the owner of the silver-grey Citroën which, she now saw, was straddling the lane, completely blocking it.

The man's eyes flicked over the English number-plate, to her face and body, and Jenni was all at once acutely aware of her dusty jeans and faded T-shirt. He advanced on her and, although she was quite tall, he towered head and shoulders over her so that, with a faint, irrational feeling almost of fear, she backed up against the side of the van, her fingers outspread behind her back, against its comforting solidity.

He looked at her, his eyes stern. Grey, she thought involuntarily, and steely-grey at that. Perhaps he chose his cars to match his eyes. But the faint smile at this flippant thought died quickly.

'Whatever you may do in England, *mademoiselle*——' he spoke in English, with only the faintest of accents, as though to underline his opinion of her abilities, but managed somehow to convey a delicately subtle insult in the words '—here in France it is not considered sensible to leave a car so near a bend.'

Jenni glanced past him, then realised that he was quite right. In the upset of the puncture, she had simply not noticed the corner, where the lane made a sharp turn between the tall hedges. If his brakes had not been so good, his reflexes so swift . . . She bit her lip at the thought of what all too easily might have happened.

'I'm sorry——' she began, but he cut her short brusquely.

'You are the owner of this——' his lip curled slightly into an expression of extreme distaste '—this vehicle?'

He gestured towards the blue and pink psychedelic dolphins that gambolled along the side of the van and, not for the first time, Jenni regretted the dubious artistic taste of Terry, the middle-aged Cornish hippy who had sold it to her the previous week for little more than he had had to pay for a new, aerodynamic surfboard. Two spots of angry colour flared in her cheeks.

'Yes, I am—I haven't stolen it, if that's what you mean.'

'Hmmm. It's merely that you appear—very young. Hardly seventeen?' He ignored her gasp of outrage. 'And yet you seem to be alone——' His gaze flicked around, as though he half expected some equally uncouth companion to come bursting through the hedge. 'Have you a driving licence?'

Jenni exploded. 'Well, of all the nerve!' It had been a very long day, and was not over yet. 'Of course I'm old enough to drive. I'm—I'm nearly nineteen and I've had a licence for—for ages.' She scowled up at him, subduing her untidy hair with an impatient gesture. 'I've said I'm sorry, and I am. What else would you like me to do, *monsieur*—grovel in the road, eat dust?'

He subjected her to a narrow-eyed, speculative look, then said coolly, 'No, merely remove your vehicle from the lane, out of my way.'

'Why? Do you own it—the lane, I mean?' Jenni instantly regretted the pert retort as his dark brows came down in a threatening frown.

'No, *mademoiselle*.' His voice was quite level. 'At least, not quite.'

She darted him a quick glance, then said, her tone a shade more placatory, 'Anyway, I can't move it at the moment. As you see, I've got a puncture.'

For a moment, remembering the fourth wheel nut she

had been wrestling with and which simply would not budge, she toyed with the tempting idea of enlisting his help, but then set her soft lips in a firm line. Very young, indeed! Never!

'If you care to wait in your car,' she said, with as much dignity as she could summon, 'I'll be as quick as I can. I've almost finished,' she added for good measure, and, leaving him to retreat, she turned her back and knelt down beside the wheel. 'Move, will you?' she whispered fiercely to the nut, and to her amazement it did.

She picked up the jack, trying to work out which way it should go. The van's instruction manual was beside her on the grass, and she was surreptitiously thumbing through the pages when all at once a pair of strong hands were under her arms and she was being forcibly lifted clear.

She tried to push at him. 'Let me go!' Her voice came out as an angry squeak as, quite unheeding, he raised her to her feet. She wrenched herself from his grip, then wheeled round to face him, her skin burning under the touch of his hands through the thin cotton of her T-shirt. 'I can do it, I tell you.'

'Oh, I'm quite sure you could, *mademoiselle*——' was there a hint of mockery in his voice? '—given the rest of the evening and most of the night as well. But you see, I happen to be in rather a hurry, so——'

He shrugged slightly, then peeled off his pale grey jacket, dropped it carelessly down on the van bonnet, deftly unknotted his silver-striped tie and tossed it on top. He squatted down on his haunches and began jacking up the vehicle.

Jenni, her feelings a hot mixture of anger and embarrassment, retreated to perch on a tussock of dusty grass, from where she watched, fascinated in spite of herself, as his large, suntanned hands worked expertly.

Her gaze wandered past him to the silver-grey car—the car which she had first seen earlier that day as she'd leaned over the ferry rail eagerly taking in the brand new sights and scents of France. The powerful-looking Citroën had swept down the hill towards the quay, to stop abruptly almost directly below her, kicking up a sharp flurry of dust from its wheels. The driver had stayed put, his face hidden from her view, while one white-shirted, gold-cufflinked arm rested negligently across the open window, and long, suntanned fingers rapped a gentle staccato against the metal.

But then, as she'd continued to gaze down, the door had opened and he'd got out. Almost as if he had sensed a pair of watching eyes on him, he had glanced up, and in the slanting rays of the early morning sunlight she'd seen a lean, tanned face, a wide, firm mouth and a square-cut jaw. The arrogant assurance, coupled with an air of slightly sardonic detachment, was evident even at that distance. A hard, ruthless man, she'd thought involuntarily.

His quick, intelligent eyes had roamed across the side of the ferry and she had moved back, a second too late, as his gaze passed her then flicked back. She had felt herself being subjected to a brief, intent survey, then, clearly dismissing her as being without further interest, his eyes had moved on, leaving her feeling faintly foolish, her cheeks flushed at the thought that he had caught her ogling him like some little schoolgirl. Well, really, he needn't have made his total uninterest quite so apparent!

Piqued, she'd watched as he had gone round to the boot and lifted out a large case and a lady's vanity-case in matching beige leather. He had set them down on the quay, then gone to the passenger door, as Jenni, having recovered her composure, continued to peer down in frank curiosity.

His companion was a tall, slim woman, her thick, fair hair cut in a short, chunky bob, and she was wearing a cream dress which even to Jenni's inexperienced eye proclaimed 'designer'.

He, meanwhile, had picked up the cases and they had walked off towards the handful of people waiting to board the ferry for its return trip to England . . .

And now, Jenni thought wonderingly, here in this remote lane in south Brittany, nearly a hundred miles from Roscoff, the ferry port where she had first seen him, this same man was now just tightening the last nut of her spare wheel. He stowed the old wheel in the boot and repacked her camping gear with a competent precision, then came over to her, wiping his fingers on an immaculate handker-chief. At the sight of those fingers, which she had studied with such intense interest that morning, an involuntary blush quickened in her cheeks. She noticed with resignation that there was not a single mark on his tight-fitting trousers, nor on the white shirt, and, all too conscious of her own grubbiness, she stood up a shade uncertainly, attempting to cover her nervousness by brushing vigorously at her jeans.

He handed her the instruction manual in silence and she smiled up at him.

'Thank you. I'm really grateful.' Then she added, with a little spurt of pride, 'Though I'm sure I could have done it myself.'

'Of course,' he agreed gravely, though she suspected that there was a spark of amusement in his eyes. He looked down at her intently, as though for the first time studying her face, but he only said, 'I hope you are not intending to drive far this evening.'

'Well, actually, I'm looking for——'

'You must not attempt to go far without a spare wheel.'

His tone was imperious. 'The garage will be closed now. You are a young girl—a foreigner—travelling alone.' His voice took on that disapproving note again and Jenni bridled at it.

'Oh, for heaven's sake, I can take care of myself perfectly well.'

He frowned angrily at her words and she knew that, again, he was right. She *was* being childishly rude in her defiance, but in ten minutes flat this total stranger had managed to antagonise her so much that she had been unable to bite back the words. All the same, she told herself, he *had* rescued her from a tricky situation. She took a deep breath.

'Well, I'm sorry, but this is the twentieth century, and surely even in France girls are allowed out alone on occasion?' Her voice was still ever so slightly fractious, so she added more mildly, 'There's no need for you to worry. I can take care of myself; really.'

He looked down at her coolly, consideringly. 'I'm sure you think you can, *mademoiselle*,' he said at last, 'but that is very far from being always the same thing. It will be dark quite soon. Suppose you were to have another puncture, what then?'

'Oh, you know the saying—lightning never strikes twice.' Jenni spoke with a confidence she was very far from feeling.

In the turmoil of the puncture and his arrival, she had temporarily put to the back of her mind the whole awful predicament she was in thanks to the mugging that afternoon in a back alley in Quimper, when she had lost her shoulder-bag containing her passport and most of her money. But now it was all oozing back in a grey sludge of fatigue, depression and worry. She had an almost overwhelming impulse to lay her head on his broad chest and pour out all her troubles to this total stranger, with the reassurance that she would never see him again, but she restrained herself just in time. He had helped her, true, but only to help himself; besides, he did not look the sort of man to overburden himself with others' woes. So, instead, she leaned against the van, biting her lip and scuffing small circles in the dust with her shoe.

'You must allow yourself to be guided by me, *mademoiselle.*' His voice was a shade softer, she thought, though there was still that imperious fibre in it, the tone of a man well used to giving orders and seeing them obeyed on the instant. 'In three kilometres you will see a tree-lined drive to your left. It leads to an excellent campsite, and tomorrow you will find a garage in the village just beyond, where they will repair your tyre.' He regarded her keenly, so that she flushed uncomfortably under the scrutiny of those penetrating grey eyes. 'Forgive me, *mademoiselle,*' he said at length, 'but you have money?'

Jenni's face crimsoned once more. 'Of course I have! 'What do you think I am?' But then, at the recollection of her situation, she went on, subduing her voice with an effort, 'Yes, I have money,' and thought to herself stoutly, well, so I have—some. Those thieves didn't quite get away with all of it.

She moved her body imperceptibly to feel the reassuring crackle of paper against her breast, and gave a faint smile of satisfaction. '. . . And remember, Jenni, always keep some of your money pinned inside your bra—you never know . . .' Thank heavens for the worldly-wise advice of her friend Rosie, the same friend who had without compunction just the previous day backed out of their joint camping trip, leaving her to face the nameless terrors of a first driving holiday in France alone.

She looked up, the smile still lingering round her lips.
'Anyway, I'm perfectly capable of looking after myself,' she
said, then, after a moment, added, 'But thank you again for
your help, *monsieur*—and I'll take your advice about the
campsite.'

She picked up his tie and jacket and held them out, but as
he took them he merely remarked, unsmilingly, 'I am
relieved that you are at last being sensible. And now,' he
continued briskly, 'if you will kindly reverse up the lane a
hundred metres or so, you will find a gateway——'

Jenni stared at him in mingled horror and disbelief.
Reversing had never been her strong point, and in a van, in
this narrow, winding lane, under the sardonic gaze of this
stranger . . .

'*Me*, reverse! Why can't you?'

He shrugged. 'It is more convenient.'

'Well, of all the nerve! What's wrong with you backing
up? If you were a gentleman, which you're obviously
not——'

'As you say, *mademoiselle*, I am not.'

It was too dark now for her to see his face clearly, but she
was quite certain that he was smiling, that faint, yet
maddeningly superior smile.

'So, as I am already late for my appointment——'

'Oh, all right, *all right*.'

Without another word, she snatched open the van door
and got in. She slammed it hard, turned on the ignition,
fumbled for the lights switch, then wrenched the lever into
reverse gear, setting her teeth in angry vexation as the
clutch grated sharply. As she turned to look over her
shoulder, she saw the Frenchman, still standing motionless
in the middle of the lane, her lights illuminating him and
casting his long, slanted shadow behind him.

She found the gateway at last and very gingerly backed into it, more than half expecting her rear wheels to lurch down into some hidden ditch. But nothing happened, and after a few moments she saw the headlights of the Citroën coming towards her. She tapped her fingers on the steering wheel, then gave a shudder of distaste as she snagged one of her nails, broken in her tussle with the wheel, against Terry's imitation tiger skin wheelcover.

There was just one thing to be grateful for, she thought sourly. The man had obviously not recognised her as the girl who had almost fallen over the ferry rail gazing rapturously down at him. That would have been truly unbearable.

He braked alongside her, but she stolidly refused to turn and face him.

'Oh, by the way,' he called, his hateful voice carrying easily over the throb of the powerful engine, 'I hope it was a calm crossing for you on the ferry last night.'

And even as Jenni's head spun round, with a last mocking wave of his hand, he was gone.

CHAPTER TWO

THE FIRST of June. Let's hope this month turns out better than the last, Jenni thought wryly as, unseen by the rest of the customers in the small pavement café, she raised her coffee-cup in a private toast.

She tried to stifle the faint pang of guilt. Having already bought coffee and a croissant earlier that morning in the attractive cafeteria at the campsite, this cup was a wholly unnecessary luxury. Still, surely she deserved a treat after the traumas of the previous day, especially the mugging, which had left her badly bruised both physically and mentally, and which now meant that she was going to have to watch every centime that she spent if she was going to be able to stay the three, maybe four days she had estimated she could now remain in France.

She wondered whether the Quimper *gendarmerie* were having any luck in tracking down her bag and, in particular, her passport. She was not at all sure how she was going to get back across the Channel without it. But, after all, what was there waiting for her? The unemployment register—the temporary hotel job in Cornwall having proved even more temporary than she'd expected? Home? No, there was no home for her to return to. Her lips tightened and she forced the unwelcome thoughts from her mind.

For this morning, at least, it was very pleasant, sitting in the shade of a lime tree, watching as a trickle of elderly women hurried into the church on the opposite side of the square, the sombre black of their dresses and cardigans a

15

strange contrast with their white lace *coiffes*, light and airy as the delicate tracery of the church steeple. From a table to her right she heard the rapid click-click as two wrinkled old men engaged in a life and death battle of dominoes. It was, she reflected, a tranquil, soothing, centuries-old scene, and it would be so easy simply to close her eyes and drift along with it for ever . . .

She was roused by a burst of laughter from inside the café. She turned and saw, seated round two tables pulled together, what was obviously a large family group. Three, no—there was a tiny baby cradled tenderly in the arms of an old lady—four generations, all in boisterously joyful mood as they celebrated some precious family occasion. As she watched, a teenage girl, clearly the centre of the festivities, was passed from one to the other, to be hugged and kissed like an adored baby herself. Jenni's heart constricted in a spasm of pain, but she thrust the familiar feeling away angrily. Surely it was time she grew up, accepted that family life for her never had been and never could be like this?

Matters had got even worse, she reflected, since her mother's premature death six months ago, after which her stepfather's total indifference to her had changed almost overnight into cold hostility. Perhaps it was understandable. Two embittered people—her mother widowed by a car crash when Jenni was barely a year old, and her stepfather, who had himself been left with a toddler when his wife had simply walked out on them. But the marriage had been a disaster, the tensions evident from the earliest days even to the ten-year-old Jenni, who had been all but ignored as the two participants had waged their silent war.

And even her young stepsister Sue—she'd never shown her more than token affection, in spite of Jenni's feelings

for her, which were born of an almost desperate need to
love something or someone . . . If only Daddy had lived, she
thought. Her father. The mugging yesterday—worse even
than the loss of her money and papers, it had deprived her
of the letter and the photograph—the only tangible links she
had with him. The letter she knew off by heart, of course,
but the photograph—how would she ever be able to hold on
to his face for the rest of her life without it?

Tears blurred her eyes suddenly, but she blinked them
away. Remember, she told herself, the questions that have
haunted you for years, eager questions that your mother
refused even to listen to, much less answer. Where your
father came from; whether any of his family were still living
in Brittany, years after his death. Although why, she asked
herself now, as she had done a hundred times since she had
impetuously planned this trip, should she have this burning
urge to discover her roots, after the heartless way he had
been treated by the very people she sought? She had no
idea, but with her mother's death that need had become
irresistible. She would seek them out, exorcise the ghosts
that had haunted her, then at last put it all behind her and
get on with her own life . . .

The mass bell tinkled and Jenni glanced at her watch.
Time to collect her tyre which she had left at the garage just
around the corner. She drained her coffee-cup and stood up,
catching for a moment her own reflection in the café
window. Thin, rather too thin. Gangling, rather than the
elegant slimness of that woman on the quay yesterday. That
untidy shock of brownish hair, matched by wide hazel eyes
and the heart-shaped face, solemn unless lit, all too rarely
these days, she thought ruefully, by an impish smile.

She paid the small bill, adding after hesitation a minute
tip for the thin-faced, rather scrawny girl who had served

her, then gathered up her small heap of purchases—comb, mirror, sunglasses, to replace those she had lost—and returned to the garage.

The enormous proprietor, clad in greasy blue denim overalls, greeted her with a beaming smile, and Jenni returned the smile with equal warmth. The garage was obviously very busy, yet when she had arrived earlier he had immediately called over a young mechanic who had been crawling around under a large Renault, and set him to work on her tyre. Now, when she dug out her thin roll of ten-franc notes from the pocket of her pink cotton sundress, he waved the money away, and when, embarrassed, she tried to insist, his giant paws closed over her hand, tightly enfolding the money.

'*Non, non, mademoiselle.*' He shook his head at her. 'Nothing to pay—no charge,' he repeated firmly, and would brook no further argument.

Oh, well, perhaps it was 'Be Kind to Foreigners' week, thought Jenni, bemused, as she drove back to the campsite. There had been no one in the office earlier, and she wanted to book two more nights.

She parked near the entrance and walked across the lawn, past attractive beds of pansies and wallflowers, to the reception block. The previous night, when she had arrived, the receptionist had barely managed to detach herself from a group of young men long enough to take her money and direct her past the caravan area to the tenting section. Jenni had intended telling her about the loss of her bag but, in the face of the girl's total indifference, and with her resolve still shaken by the encounter in the lane, she had merely paid her money and retreated.

Outside reception, a large caravan attached to an English car was drawn up, and inside were a young, rather helpless-looking couple, two grizzling toddlers clutching at their knees. There was no sign of the girl, only a harassed-looking, middle-aged woman whom Jenni had seen earlier that morning serving breakfasts in the cafeteria. She was staring, as though hypnotised, into a computer screen filled with a complicated array of figures, and when she caught sight of Jenni she burst into a gesticulating flood of French, clearly imploring her for help.

Without allowing herself time to think, Jenni gave the holiday-makers a warm, reassuring smile. 'Can I help you?'

'Thank God—somebody who speaks English.' The man's strained face broke into a beam of pure relief. 'You see, miss, there seems to be a problem over our pre-paid vouchers.'

For the next few minutes, Jenni found herself acting as liaison officer, translating between the two sides of the counter and untangling the mystic symbols on the computer screen. She was actually beginning to enjoy herself when, as she turned to the couple, she saw out of the corner of her eye a man leaning, arms folded, against an open doorway at the far end of the reception area, and at the sight of him she dropped the forms she was holding. The man was in deep shadow and half hidden by a towering potted palm, but there was no mistaking the stranger she had encountered the previous day, even though he was dressed now, not in formal clothes, but in a pale blue silky sweater and tight, grey casual trousers.

So, after all, their paths had crossed again. He must, unlikely as it seemed, also be staying here. If that was the case, could she bear to stay on herself, or would she have to spend more of her precious francs moving on to another site? Her frustration was compounded by a flicker of nervousness. How long, she wondered, had he been standing there, a silent, interested spectator? She stooped to pick up the sheets of paper, glad to escape from his eyes, for she knew, with a sudden anger, that her colour had risen. She simply mustn't allow him the satisfaction of seeing that he had disconcerted her again.

She straightened up and, forcing herself to ignore his disturbing presence, finished filling in the forms, tore off the duplicates and handed them back across the desk to the couple. She pointed them in the direction of the hard-standing caravan area, and explained where to find the camp supermarket and the shower blocks, set back among a screen of trees and shrubs.

Although she had deliberately not even glanced in his direction again, she knew—felt—with every quivering fibre of her body, that the man was still there, silently watching her, and as soon as the young family, fulsomely grateful, had gone, she herself smilingly brushed aside the torrent of thanks from the Frenchwoman and made rapidly for the door.

'Do not run away just yet, Mademoiselle Green.'

How on earth did he know her name? He must have checked on her in the camp visitors' book. How dared he? Jenni's hackles rose but, none the less his voice, low but authoritative, stopped her in her tracks and she swung round, her mouth tightening as he sauntered up to her.

'I don't know what you do in France, *monsieur*,' she said sweetly, giving the final words a light emphasis, the memory of their last meeting still rankling, 'but in England it is considered very ill-mannered to read a private guest register.'

His dark brows contracted threateningly, and as he took another step towards her Jenni clasped her hands together to still their trembling. But, before he could reply, the other woman broke in with a rapid volley of colloquial French, almost totally incomprehensible to Jenni, but, she realised, addressed to 'Monsieur Raoul'.

Monsieur Raoul? Jenni's eyes widened and she stared at him, appalled. Was he——? No, surely he wasn't, couldn't be, anything other than a camper like herself? She had just made up her mind that she would not allow herself to be frightened off—that she would stay on here for the few days that remained—but if he really was an employee there would be even less chance of avoiding him.

She inched her way towards the exit, hoping to slip away unnoticed, but the man suddenly turned and gestured imperiously to her to remain. He broke into the flow of gabbled speech, politely but with a hint of impatience, steered the woman towards a rear door and closed it firmly behind her. Then he motioned Jenni towards the open door where he had been standing.

'Come into the office, Mademoiselle Green.'

She swallowed nervously. 'I——' she began, but he only repeated, a remnant of that barely contained impatience in his voice, 'Come this way, please.'

She opened her mouth to argue. The thought of another enforced confrontation in which she would again inevitably come off second best did not in the least appeal to her, but then, after shooting him another sideways glance, she thought better of defiance. Without doubt, she realised with a tremor, he would, if provoked, snatch her up under one arm and carry her through that door.

She affected a poise she was far from feeling and, glancing down at her watch, said, 'Very well, I can spare you a few minutes.'

'I'm so grateful.' His tone was unmistakably ironic, but she did not allow herself to react to the provocation in it, and walked past him.

The office was comfortably furnished. A large, old, polished table served as a desk, littered with papers and folders and an electric typewriter. He pulled across a low leather chair and gestured her to it, before sitting at the desk. He regarded her for some moments in silence until Jenni, ill at ease under the intense scrutiny of those grey eyes, began fidgeting with the brass studs on the upholstered arm. He had no doubt done it deliberately: put her in this ridiculously low modern armchair, so that she was forced to sit hunched in it, with her knees almost up to her chin and gazing up at him, almost—almost as though she was kneeling in supplication to him.

'You did not tell me that you speak French.' His voice cut through the silence of the room and she shrugged.

'You didn't ask.' Then, with the stinging recollection of his behaviour, she added, 'I suppose you assumed that because I was driving a beat-up old van and wearing dirty clothes that I had to be some kind of mindless moron.'

She looked up at him, momentarily fearful of the effect her words might have on him, but a faint smile flickered round his lips. 'You have a ready tongue, *mademoiselle*—which leads me on to the reason I wished to see you. Claudette was singing your praises just now, and I heard enough myself to realise that for a young girl you were dealing remarkably efficiently with that English family.' When Jenni tried to speak, he silenced her with a wave of his hand. 'How long were you intending to stay at Les Forêts, Mademoiselle Green?'

'Well——' Jenni hesitated, then went on, deliberately vague, 'I haven't quite decided. Two or three nights, I think.'

'And then moving on? That is unfortunate.'

He subjected her to a long, speculative look, until her former discomfort returned. Whatever did he mean? Was he going to offer her some reward for her help—an additional night for free, perhaps?

'You see, *mademoiselle*, we find ourselves in—how shall I put it?—in a slight predicament this morning. Marie-Christine, our young receptionist, left hurriedly in the middle of the night, in company, I gather, with some young men who had been camping here.'

'Oh, dear, I'm sorry.'

He gave her a wry smile. 'Save your sympathy for Marie-Christine—and her new friends. Her father, our village butcher, has gone in search of them . . .' He spread his hands graphically. 'Marie-Christine was, let us say, not an angel, but she worked here last season and knows her job—typing, answering queries, working our computer and so on.'

He picked up a pen and, as Jenni watched in fascination, began turning it over and over between his fingers. His hands were large, capable-looking, strong, yet the long fingers, tapering to carefully manicured nails, subtly conveyed also the impression of delicacy, even sensitivity . . .

She tore her eyes away and saw that he was watching her. His gaze was bland, but she had the uneasy sensation that he read her mind, though he only said, 'Yes, despite her deficiences, Marie will be difficult to replace. However, perhaps we have a neat solution at hand. Do you speak other languages?'

Jenni was startled by the suddenness of the question. 'Y-yes. At least,' she added warily, 'I scraped through O-Level in German. Oh, and I picked up quite a bit of Spanish from a girl I was working with in——'

'And have you a situation in England?'

'Well, n-no,' she admitted with great reluctance. She felt sure that to this hard-eyed man unemployment would somehow be a sign of inefficiency, weakness even. 'I had one—in a hotel, for a couple of months, but I lost it last week.' She hesitated again, then fearing that her statement was too bald, as though she might have been caught pocketing the teaspoons, she added, 'You see, the weather was awful, and anyway, the hotel was taken over by new owners and they——'

'So you have worked in a hotel. And what did you do before that?'

Jenni stared at him. Was he going to take her through the whole of her dull, uninteresting life? But somehow she felt compelled to answer him.

'Well, I left school at sixteen,' she said flatly.

'But you clearly have a certain flair for language— your French accent is very pure, for an English girl. And you have German. Why did you not pursue your studies?'

Jenni gave him a rueful half-smile, remembering her stepfather's reaction to her final, encouraging school report, and her tentatively expressed hope that she might go on to the local college. Unbidden, the bleak images arose of the ensuing three years, of short periods of employment in dead-end jobs, and frequent, longer periods of unemployment. The training course in hotel work had seemed at the time a last resort, but she had come to love her job in the Cornish hotel, believing that at last she had reached a turning-point for the better, but then . . .

'It just didn't seem possible,' she said at last, with a faint shrug. 'But when I get home, I'm hoping——'

He interrupted her with a peremptory gesture. 'So, you have no employment now.' He eyed her for a moment, then went on musingly, 'That explains why you have the look of poverty.'

Jenni gave a gasp of outrage and stared at him, very pale. 'How dare you insult me like this? I don't know w-who the hell you think you are, but I've a good mind to—to report you to your boss . . .' Angry tears were very near the surface now. 'And I'm not staying here a moment longer.'

She braced herself to get up out of the squashy chair, but before she could move he was round the desk. He put his hands on her shoulders and gave her a none-too-gentle shove back down into it. She struggled against his hands, then subsided, glowering at him as he leaned against the desk.

'Let us be quite clear about this, *mademoiselle*. I bring this interview to a close, not you. Do you understand?'

Jenni, still glowering, could only nod speechlessly.

'Do not bridle at me when I tell you the truth,' he continued. 'To me you have the appearance of a young girl who has never in her whole life been able to spend money freely on herself—on clothes . . .' His eyes raked casually, almost cruelly, over the simple pink sundress, and all at once Jenni was bitterly aware of the cheap, flimsy cotton, the bodice which did not sit perfectly, because the material had been a sale remnant, and there had not been quite enough of it when she had come to make it up. '. . . on hair . . .' and she was acutely conscious of the shaggy remains of the previous winter's perm, which she should really have had lopped off '. . . and so, by offering you Marie-Christine's position here, I am doing you a great favour.'

Marie-Christine's position? A job—here? Dazed, Jenni could only repeat his words.

'Yes. That is, if your parents have no objection.'

'Oh, my parents are dead.' She spoke mechanically, her

mind whirling. The abruptly made offer had almost
stunned her, and her first instinct was a blunt refusal. But
as she stared at him, the whole crazy idea began to seem,
first faintly possible, then inviting, even exciting. From the
little she had seen of the area, the campsite was set in
pleasant countryside, near the sea . . . and yes, she pursed
her lips, she certainly could do with the money, though she
would die rather than admit as much to him. She could
regard it as a working holiday . . . although, on second
thoughts, if Monsieur Raoul—she sneaked him a quick
look, but he seemed intent on some papers in front of
him—had very much to do with it, it would be considerably
more working than holiday. He was a bred-in-the-bone
slave-driver, if ever she'd set eyes on one. But what was
there for her to rush home for? The dole, the possibly
fruitless search for another job? And besides, if she did stay
on at Les Forêts, it would give her more time to find out
about her father's family . . .

'I should perhaps have mentioned that the salary is
excellent. Also, as an estate employee, you will move out of
that wretched little tent——' he really had been checking up
on her, she thought grimly, but bit back her retort '—and
will take over Marie-Christine's *appartement*. You will, of
course, take your meals in the cafeteria.'

He was speaking, she thought, with a quick flash of
resentment, as though her acceptance of the job, and any
conditions he might care to impose, was a foregone
conclusion—as it doubtless was to him. If ever there was a
man who expected others to fall in, tame as mice, with his
plans for their future, whatever their own feelings . . . No, it
was more than that, she realised, with a shiver of
unease—he was not even allowing for the possibility that
she might have any feelings, any will of her own . . .

Was it, after all, such a brilliant idea, this job? Presumably, as fellow employees, they would be in constant contact, and already, Jenni acknowledged, although he was being very formal with her, his potent physical attractiveness was working a kind of alchemy in her, so that even when, as now, she was looking down at her tightly interlaced hands lying primly in her lap, she was vibrantly aware of his every move . . .

'Of course, there will be a few formalities to complete. May I have your passport?'

'Oh, no!' Jenni started up in alarm. 'I—I mean—that's not possible,' she added lamely. For some obscure reason, she did not want to tell him about the mugging. Perhaps it would be possible to stall him, at least for a few days, to give the *gendarmerie* a chance, and until she had proved that she could do the job anyway.

'It is essential that I have your passport,' he repeated firmly.

No, it would not be possible. 'You can't,' she replied flatly. 'I—I've lost it.' And when he raised his dark brows interrogatively, she continued, 'You see, yesterday afternoon I was looking round Quimper . . .'

And she told him how, in the lunch-time quiet of the old market town, three youths had followed her into that high-walled alley, had without warning set upon her, pushing her roughly to the ground and, as she lay dazed, had snatched the bag from her helpless hands . . .

He listened to her story in silence, leaning back in his chair, and when she finished he gave no exclamations of horror or sympathy, only said quietly, '*Mademoiselle*, you are very brave. No, it is true,' as she coloured in surprise, 'faced with that appalling situation, most young girls, I am quite certain, would have returned immediately to the ferry port, in a flood of self-pitying tears.'

Jenni pulled a face and laughed. 'Well, to be honest, I did think of it—going home, I mean.'

'But you did not. And now I will show you your *appartement*, before I ring the *gendarmerie*.'

He straightened up and went over to the door.

'Oh, there's no need,' Jenni said. 'Thank you, but I've already informed them, and I'm sure nothing can be done, anyway.' Although, looking at him, she was maybe not quite so sure, after all. If anyone could track down her missing bag, it was this man. 'But if they do find it, perhaps you would let me know, so that I can collect it.'

He watched her cross the room to him. 'Have you never been here before, *mademoiselle?* We have had several groups of young English Girl Guide campers in previous years—you were among them, I think?'

'Oh, no, I've never been out of England before.'

'And yet—there is something . . .' He spoke almost as though to himself. 'Your natural grace, the way you hold your head . . .' In her confusion, Jenni stumbled into a low table and his eyes glinted for a moment in genuine amusement. 'Oh, do not be embarrassed, *mademoiselle*. You must learn to accept compliments.'

'Mmm.' Jenni had recovered her poise. 'Though it's a pity about the clothes and hair, *n'est-ce pas, monsieur?*'

Her reply obviously caught him by surprise, and he smiled spontaneously. He should smile more often, thought Jenni fleetingly, it changes his whole face. He held up a hand in protest.

'Please, not *"monsieur"*. A pleasantly informal working relationship is so much more preferable, don't you agree, Jenni?'

It was the first time that he had used her first name, and

the faintly foreign inflexion he gave to it seemed to cast a glow of exotic allure over the down-to-earth English name. Even so, she did not agree, not in the slightest—for her own peace of mind, their relationship must be allowed only to remain on the most formal of levels. But she remained silent and he went on, 'So, at least when we are alone, it is Raoul. And now, your *appartement* . . .'

As he opened the car door for her, he casually remarked that someone would take down her tent, pack it into the van and bring them round to the staff area. When she tried to point out that she was quite capable—and anyway *preferred* to do it herself—he brushed her protest aside, so she merely sank back into the upholstered leather, still struggling to come to terms with the fact that she was actually riding in the sleek grey beast which, just the day before, she had gazed down on from the ferry rail.

The narrow, dusty drive wound between clumps of trees and massive rhododendron bushes. Raoul handled the car as though it had just leapt from the Le Mans starting grid, so that she involuntarily closed her eyes several times and jabbed her foot down on an imaginary brake. So his precipitate arrival in the lane the previous evening had not been a temporary aberration.

'There is something wrong?' His voice held a hint of dry amusement.

'No,' she said, keeping her eyes on the windscreen. 'I was just wondering if all Frenchmen drive like utter lunatics, or whether you're something special.'

'Well, we all drive like madmen,' he replied carelessly, 'but I must leave you to decide whether I am—something special.' She glanced at him, not quite sure how to take this, but he continued, 'So you can relax, Jenni——' Jenni again,

and again that uneasy, yet almost delicious shiver '—you are
quite safe in my hands.'

Ah, but am I? The disquieting question rose disconcert-
ingly in her mind. His hand, reaching for her seat-belt, had
casually brushed across her breast, then slid down past her
thigh as he locked it into position, and even now, minutes
later, she could still feel an uncomfortable warmth on her
skin.

The drive at last widened out, first to fields, then lawns.
Down an alley of high, clipped yews, Jenni caught a
glimpse of a pinkish stone, grey slate-roofed manor house,
its façade masked by a mass of golden and white climbing
roses. The house was small, yet somehow its beauty was
wholly satisfying, and Jenni clutched her hands together in
delight.

'Oh, what a beautiful house! Do stop, please,' she gasped,
and Raoul slowed for a few seconds. 'Those pretty towers at
each end—it's like a fairy-tale castle. I can just imagine
Rapunzel living in one of them, and letting her hair down
for the prince——' She broke off, suddenly aware of his
eyes, not on the house, but on her, and finished lamely, 'It's
really lovely.'

He slipped the car into gear and pulled away. 'It's the
Château Les Forêts—the heart of the estate.'

'Oh, so the people who own the house also own the
camping-site.'

'Yes.'

'And you manage it for them.'

'Yes, I manage it.'

The drive ran behind a high granite wall and Jenni
turned in her seat for a last look at the house. She thought of
the succession of mean little flats where she had spent most
of her life.

'Mmm, I hope they know just how lucky they are.'

'Lucky? Oh—I think so,' he said briefly. 'Look, through there in the old walled garden is the swimming pool. It is part of the site facilities, but staff are permitted to swim there at quiet times.'

He pulled into a cobbled courtyard where a couple of peacocks were scratching around among the huge tubs of petunias, for all the world like a pair of farmyard hens.

'These are the old stables—the new stable block is behind the château. Your *appartement* is over here.'

He led the way to a flight of narrow stone steps, worn down in the middle by centuries of use, and Jenni could only follow him, quite dazed. It was as if she was caught up in an old silent movie, where everything and everyone moved at a heightened, unreal speed. Raoul ran lightly up the steps and turned to face her outside a blue-painted door.

'By the way, your tyre has been repaired, I trust?'

'Oh, yes, thank you.'

Jenni was slightly breathless, and not only from trotting up the steps behind him. The energy and drive of this man left her feeling faintly unsteady. Now they were standing very close together on the tiny square of landing, and instinctively she took a step back, fetching up against the wooden safety rail.

'Good. René was very busy, but he said he would manage it.'

He dug a key-ring out of his pocket, unlocked the blue door and gestured her inside. But Jenni stood staring at him, as the import of his words sank into her brain like lead . . . No charge . . . 'Be Kind to Foreigners' week . . . Just how naïve could you possibly get? A garage chock full of cars under repair, and you get the red carpet treatment for one miserable puncture! Of course, Raoul had fixed it, as he had now fixed her job. Was there anything he couldn't or wouldn't manipulate if it suited him? She looked up at him, trying to meet the steel-grey eyes without flinching.

'You paid for it, didn't you?'

'No, I just told René to put it on my account,' he said airily.

'You told him——! And what will he think, do you imagine?' she said, the impotent fury rising in her.

'He will think nothing. He is not paid to think—so he will not.'

Jenni bunched her hands in the pockets of her sundress. 'I can't possibly allow you,' she said stiffly. 'You must let me pay you. I—I insist.'

'Oh, what a prim little English miss!' He laughed, not altogether pleasantly. 'I'll deduct it from your first week's wages. Does that suit you?'

'Perfectly, thank you,' she replied formally, and walked past him.

The apartment was dark, the air fetid and heavy with a cheap, cloying perfume. Raoul gave an exclamation of distaste, strode across to the shutters and flung them open, so that fresh air and light poured in. He looked round, at the overflowing waste-paper basket, the pieces of lipstick-smeared tissue, sordid chunks of cotton wool, lying beside an almost empty pot of thick face-cream. Beyond was a tiny bathroom; someone had tossed a half-empty bottle of hair colourant across the shower tray and left it to congeal in ugly reddish smears, while the basin was choked with dried soapsuds and long black hairs.

'*Mon Dieu*, what a mess!' Raoul was looking round him in utter disgust. 'The filthy little——' He used a word in French which Jenni had never heard, but its general import reached her.

'Don't worry,' she said. 'I've worked as a chambermaid and, believe me, you'd be surprised at the sights you see in respectable hotel bedrooms! I'll soon deal with this. And at least she made her bed before she went.'

Raoul laughed shortly. 'Oh, I don't think our little alley cat spent many nights here! This bed probably hasn't been slept in for weeks. But you will not clear out her filth—one of the maids from the château will do it. I want you back down at the camp office.'

'Ay, ay, sir!' The mock salute slipped out before she could stop herself.

Raoul studied her thoughtfully. 'Mmm. I think that perhaps you are not the ordinary, demure little *Anglaise* I took you for. There is a spark of spirit in those hazel eyes . . .'

He took a step towards her and Jenni, trapped between him and the bed, was unable to move. Very slowly, almost leisurely, his hands came up and his fingers brushed across her cheek. He lightly ran his thumb across the pulse in her neck and out along the smooth line of her shoulder to the edge of her sundress, then traced the neckline across the swell of her breasts.

Jenni, her flesh quivering, stood with head bent, terrified lest he should hear—or feel—the erratic beating of her heart, her shallow, unsteady breathing. Under the hypnotic influence of that casual, slow-moving thumb, she half closed her eyes, and felt herself sway slightly towards him, but then her eyes flew open. What was she doing? The whole crazy morning had infected her brain, made her crazy, too!

Furious with herself, she jerked back from him. 'Don't do that,' she said coldly, though a treacherous tremor made her voice unsteady. 'I don't know whether you think that as the manager you've got—what do you call it?—*droit de seigneur,* or something, over all the female employees——'

He dropped his hand to his side, his face darkening with anger, so that she quailed, but then, terrified by her own temerity, she rushed on, 'Because if so, you're going to be disappointed in me. So maybe Marie-Christine is a little good-for-nothing. Perhaps you have good reason to know that——' she heard him take a sharp, angry breath '—but I'm n-not like that.'

She went to push past him, but he put both hands on her waist and whirled her back, catching her to him and smothering her frantic struggles against his broad chest. Then he thrust her away from him, but the shock made her gasp out loud.

'You—you overgrown bully!'

Still breathing deeply, he held her gaze for several moments, then said roughly, 'Never speak to me like that again.'

He let her past him this time, and she stumbled blindly down the stairway, leaving him to relock the door. She leaned up against the car, and by the time he sauntered up to her, hands in pockets, she had managed to assume a forced nonchalance.

'Oh, by the way,' he said, 'you will need a key.'

He took out the key-ring, slipped off one of the two keys, and handed it to her. She coolly thanked him, inwardly relieved that her voice was now quite under control. He casually thrust the other key back into his pocket, then, seeing her eyes follow his action, said, 'Don't be alarmed. I'm sure you will appreciate that as the—manager, I must have a duplicate key for every door on the estate.'

Aghast, Jenni gaped at him. 'You mean—that's another key to my apartment?'

'Of course.'

His eyes dared her to make a scene, in front of a group of ebullient young campers who had just appeared, clutching towels and swimsuits, but, folding her lips on her reply, she got into the car and sat in silence as he drove back to the office . . .

The cafeteria was deserted when Jenni opened the glass door. Inside, although the furnishings were utilitarian, the white lattice-effect plastic chairs, the brown and muted terracotta of the floor tiles, the sea prints in soft pastels on the walls, gave the long room a cool, tranquil air after the early afternoon heat in the courtyard. The teenage waitress brought her pâté, a plate of cold sliced beef and salad, and a piece of apple tart, together with some hunks of bread and a half-bottle of red wine. Then, to Jenni's relief, she disappeared through the bead curtain behind the counter, presumably to her own meal.

She needed to be on her own for a while. No talking, no smiling—her jaw ached with smiling, and her head throbbed with the effect of high-speed thinking on her feet—and in French, too, with Monsieur Raoul never, it seemed, absent for long. She poured herself a glass of wine, then pushed the remainder away, reflecting that her bright new competent image would receive a severe dent if she was found snoring under the office table by mid-afternoon, and leaned back in her chair, still feeling faintly dazed. Maybe she ought to pinch herself; surely she must have dreamed it all? At eight that morning she had been sitting at that table over there, eating a croissant and staring into a bleak, uncertain future. Now, just hours later, she was a fully-fledged employee of Les Forêts, recovering from a frenetic morning . . .

The bead curtain rustled and the young waitress put her

head through.

'*Café*, Mademoiselle Jenni?'

When she put down the cup, she said, 'So you are to have Marie-Christine's apartment. We're all glad she's gone.'

Jenni stirred her coffee, then asked carefully, 'Why was she kept on if she was so unsatisfactory? Was it perhaps that she and Monsieur Raoul——?' She broke off and gave a delicately expressive shrug.

'That she was Monsieur Raoul's mistress, you mean?' The girl gave a snort of derisive laughter. 'Hardly—when he can have the pick of the local women. They're all mad for him,' she added, with the wordly wisdom of fifteen. 'Besides, there is Hélène Marquand. He——' She broke off suddenly, as though recollecting that Jenni, though a fellow employee, was a newcomer and therefore not to be treated—at least yet—to the juicier details, then added, 'Marie-Christine wasn't bad at her job—quite good, really.'

Jenni thoughtfully took a sip of the strong, aromatic coffee. 'Are there other staff apartments in the old stable block, besides mine?'

'Oh, yes, they're all there.'

Jenni's heart sank. Raoul, with his duplicate key to her apartment, living next door perhaps, one thin partition wall between them.

'And Monsieur Raoul—does—does he live there as well?'

'But of course not!' The girl laughed, and Jenni's spirits lifted a notch. A house in the village, that was infinitely safer, although she dared not ask herself why that should be.

'He lives in the château, of course. Since Madame—his adoptive mother—died, he lives alone. At least——' She broke off with a knowing grin then, catching sight of Jenni's puzzled expression, looked searchingly at her. 'So he didn't tell you?'

'Tell me what?' Jenni felt a sudden, inexplicable stab of alarm.

'Why, that he is the owner—of the château, Les Forêts—everything.'

CHAPTER THREE

JENNI towelled herself roughly, then flopped down on the grass beside the deserted swimming pool. She oiled herself, noting with satisfaction her rapidly deepening tan, and lay back on her towel, grateful to have finished work for the day.

The job, like any in the services industry, was hard and taxing, but now, at the end of her first week, she knew the ropes and was enjoying the work more than anything she had ever done. For the first time in her life she was not being constantly put down, disregarded, and she realised almost with surprise that she was relishing the responsibility, gaining quickly in self-confidence.

During the first couple of days Raoul had seemed omnipresent. She had caught distant glimpses of him, striding energetically about the site, a feathery borzoi hound constantly trotting at his heels. More frequently, he was in the reception area, no doubt reassuring himself, she'd thought ironically, that his spur of the moment decision to employ her had not been a monumental error. And perhaps that had been the main reason why she had approached her work so wholeheartedly. She certainly did not intend to give him the minutest opportunity to find fault with her, for even though the entire staff seemed to adore 'Monsieur Raoul' unreservedly, she felt certain that, where she at any rate was concerned, the slightest lapse would provoke a caustic rebuke.

Still, even as he'd watched her, he had mercifully stayed

on the periphery—and Jenni, her nerve-endings quivering
at this nearness, had told herself that she was glad of this;
while his few direct contacts with her had been formal, even
cool.

Even so, she had experienced a strange feeling of
emptiness when, on the third morning, Claudette
mentioned that he had gone down to the south-west—
trouble at the family vineyard, estate gossip had hinted
vaguely. Jenni had first registered shock that on top of the
well-heeled estate there was also a vineyard, then thrown
herself headlong into her work, to drown that faint, yet
disquieting sensation of being bereft of something . . .

She rolled over on to her stomach, tugged up a blade of
coarse grass, and chewed it absent-mindedly. Raoul. At the
mere thought of his name, she could still feel a tremor, a
faint reverberation of the shock-waves that had raced
through her at the waitress's wholly unexpected revelation.
She had just about resigned herself to his being the manager
of Les Forêts, but the knowledge that he was the owner . . .
Her first instinctive reaction had been sheer horror that she
had been so pert with him . . . 'I don't know whether you
think you've got *droit de seigneur*, or something' . . . Jenni
groaned inwardly, and for the umpteenth time blushed at
the shaming memory, but then the image of Raoul's darkly
handsome face as he roughly pulled her to him slid
insidiously into her mind and she involuntarily closed her
eyes against the sudden stab of painful recollection.

Earlier, as she'd had a swim, she had thought contentedly
how this place was entwining itself around her. Could it be,
though, that it was not Les Forêts that was busy encircling
her heart, but its absent owner? Surely not, and yet——
Come on, my girl, she told herself scornfully. Falling for
the boss, are we? This won't do. A holiday romance

was dangerous enough—a working holiday romance could be even more of a cataclysmic disaster . . . Perhaps when she had had her meal, instead of the boring early night she had planned, she would change and, after all, meet up with that young camper whose pressing invitations she had been smilingly refusing for the past three days. Yes, she would stroll down with him to the village and spend a pleasant evening at the open-air café, watching the men play boules under the lengthening shade of the lime trees.

As she dug in her bag for her comb, her fingers brushed against the small brown envelope. Her first pay day! What were aching legs and a slight headache brought on by dealing with a couple of difficult tourists who had arrived two days ahead of their booking date, compared with all those lovely crackling fifty-franc notes? If the job lasted through the season she would, with free board and lodging, be taking home a really substantial nest egg against the bleak fear of a winter's unemployment.

Yes, after all the traumas of that first day in Brittany, things were working out very nicely. True, she was as far as ever from finding out about her father's family. So far, she had just not had the time—but anyway, they might well have moved away or be dead. After all, it had been nearly twenty years ago . . .

She sat up and pulled on her blue T-shirt over her bikini top, her eyes remote. Perhaps, after all, it didn't really matter; she was Jenni Green, not Jenni Kerouac, and in the long run—she wriggled into her jeans, and slid her feet into the new pink espadrilles she had treated herself to that morning in the camp supermarket—in the long run, surely what mattered was she herself. Perhaps it was best to let those famous sleeping dogs lie.

*   *   *

'Jenni, where have you been?' Claudette looked up from the till as the cafeteria door swung to. 'Monsieur Raoul wishes to see you!'

So he was back. A feeling of intense, breathless elation filled her, so that she wanted to stand on tiptoe. Still, she forced herself to stroll unconcernedly across the empty room.

'He has been searching for you for an hour. He went up to your *appartement,* but you were not there.'

Claudette's good-natured face looked flustered, almost accusing.

'Oh, I walked through the campsite to check that everything was all right, then I had a swim,' Jenni said, as casually as she could against the rapid pit-pat of her heart.

'He wishes to see you,' Claudette repeated. Then, as Jenni dropped her bag on to a chair, added in consternation, 'At once, he said—as soon as you were found.'

Well, really! Anyone would think she was a medieval serf, poised to leap at the crack of an—only just—invisible whip. Still, it would certainly be unwise to disobey. Raoul was clearly in a bad mood after a long, hot drive up from Bordeaux—and, after all, she admitted unwillingly, however much she might try to pretend otherwise, she was consumed with impatience to see him once again. She picked up her bag.

'Is he in the office?'

'Oh, no, he is waiting for you at the château. You are to go to the front entrance and ring the bell.'

The château? Jenni stared at her and a cold finger of unease, almost apprehension, touched her mind. Whatever crime had she unwittingly committed? She felt suddenly an overpowering certainty that this was why she had been so formally summoned. Perhaps—her stomach lurched—

perhaps she was to be dismissed? She swallowed down a
hard lump in her throat; she had grown to love her work,
and besides—— She bit her lip, then, seeing Claudette's
curious, even speculative eyes on her, pulled herself
together.

'Oh, well,' she shrugged, with a weak attempt at
insouciance, 'I'll be back later for my meal.'

The château was even prettier than Jenni had imagined
from her brief glimpses, with the soft, slightly blurred
beauty of a romantic film set. The evening sunlight had
turned the walls to a translucent rosy pink, while along the
wide terrace the grey granite slabs had a silvered lightness.
On the gravel, at the front of the flight of shallow stone
steps which led up to the portico, the grey Citroën was
parked, and Jenni, feeling a sudden need to assert herself,
pulled up her battered van a thumb's breadth from the
gleaming rear bumper.

She switched off the engine and sat quite still for a few
moments. Raoul. In spite of her nervousness over the
imminent interview, her heart fluttered unevenly at the
prospect of seeing him again, and when she glanced in the
driving mirror, her reflection, though faintly apprehensive,
was rose-flushed, the eyes brilliant and starry. Too
revealing by half, my girl, she thought ironically, and tried
to wipe it clear of all emotion. Her hair, still damp from her
swim, hung in a disordered mass, so she tucked it in firmly
behind her ears, then got out and walked briskly up the
steps.

Beside the large old front door a stone lion stood guard,
his muzzle worn by years of weather and children's
caresses, Jenni guessed as, almost unthinkingly, she ran her
own fingers lightly over the sun-warmed head, then gave

the ornate brass bell-pull a tug. It echoed just for a second somewhere inside the house, then the door was opened by a uniformed maid, so promptly that Jenni suspected, again with that twinge of unease, that she had been hovering in the hall, awaiting her arrival.

The entrance hall was large and airy, the black and white marble floor-tiles gleaming faintly against rugs which, though old, still glowed with colour, while the azure ceiling—Jenni raised her eyes momentarily—was gilded and painted in the rococo style, with fat, sly cherubs frisking around buxom nymphs.

She followed the maid along a passage, hearing the incongruous flap-flap of her rope-soled espadrilles on the highly polished wood, and hoping desperately that she appeared more composed than she felt. The maid knocked at a door, half opened it, gestured Jenni past her, then retreated hastily down the passage.

Jenni, butterflies fluttering madly around the pit of her stomach, took a deep breath and put her hand to the door, feeling her palm moist against the panel. This was ridiculous. Pull yourself together, she thought angrily; he can only dismiss you, he can't eat you—quite. She pushed the door open and went in.

She was vaguely aware that the room was beautiful, long and high-ceilinged, that the green silk wallpaper perfectly matched the background shade of the old, flowered carpet, that every piece of highly polished furniture was exactly right, every piece of delicately tinted porcelain perfect. Even the silky-haired borzoi stretched out by the empty hearth seemed to harmonise with the setting. Yet, even as her brain somehow registered all this, and the scent of roses, perhaps drifting in through the tall, half-open windows, she was only conscious of Raoul.

He had not even changed since his return, for his tie and
the jacket to his lightweight silver-grey suit had been
carelessly thrown down across an armchair. Now, he was
leaning against the huge, ornate marble fireplace, his arms
folded, eyes watching her, his face expressionless. There
was a new, remote, even forbidding quality about him, and
Jenni, conscious suddenly of an unnerving, almost
frightening tension in the room, swallowed down a spasm
of fear. Still, she forced her unwilling legs across the miles
of carpet, soft as woodland moss under her dusty
espadrilles.

'You—you sent for me.' She was aware of the faint tremor
in her voice.

Raoul did not reply directly. He gestured towards a table,
and Jenni, her eyes following his pointing finger, gave a
gasp of delight.

'Oh, my bag! How marvellous.'

She almost ran over to the table and snatched up the
shoulder-bag. One of the cheap gilt clasps had been
wrenched off, but otherwise it seemed none the worse.

'It was found in a culvert on the outskirts of Quimper.'

Jenni, intent on her bag, only half registered the Arctic
chill in Raoul's voice.

'But—but I don't understand. Why was it brought
here—to the château, I mean?'

He shrugged. 'I contacted the local *gendarmerie*—asked
them to lean on their colleagues in Quimper a little. I
suppose it was then natural for the officer to bring it here to
me.'

'So I have you to thank for finding it.'

The overpowering relief made her feel almost light-
headed—not only had she got back her precious bag, but
her fears over Raoul's summons had been totally,

ridiculously unfounded. She gave him a sparkling smile, but that cold, watchful hostility was evident still on his face. What was wrong? Jenni did not know, could not even guess, so she turned back to the bag and began riffling through it.

'Any money it once contained has, of course, gone.'

'Oh, never mind the money,' Jenni said absently, her fingers flicking through the crowded contents in increasing anxiety. Comb—make-up—empty purse—they were all intact, but . . . Oh, please let them be here, she thought.

'This is perhaps what you are seeking?'

At the hard note in his voice, she put down the bag and turned slowly, then saw, on a low table, set out as though for her approval, a dark blue passport, and a crumpled envelope and photograph. She gave a gasp of pure relief.

'Oh, yes, they're mine,' she said, but as she went to gather them up, Raoul's hand closed over her wrist. With his other hand, he reached across, picked up the passport and flicked it open. He thrust it in front of her face.

'This is you—Eugénie Aimée Green?'

Jenni's eyes flew from the passport to his face, set in hard, cold lines.

'I—I——' Then, as he shook her wrist angrily, she faltered, 'Y—yes, but I'm always called Jenni. No one ever calls me Eugénie—I don't like the name,' she added flatly.

The tension in the room, smothering and incomprehensible, was winding itself around her, and she forced herself to make a huge effort to break free of it. She ran the tip of her tongue round her dry lips.

'Look, Raoul, if it's about the mix-up over that booking this morning, I——' she began, but he broke in with a furious exclamation.

'Do not try to be naïve with me, you little——'

He bit back the word, and gave her a push which sent her reeling against a tall-backed chair, to stare up at him, totally bewildered, as the colour drained from her face. He was clearly very angry; she felt his fury lashing her, although after that one quick blow he had dropped the passport and retreated to lean against the fireplace again, his hands thrust deep into his pockets, as though afraid of his own feelings.

Somehow, Jenni made herself speak, though she could hardly trust her own voice. 'I don't know what you're talking about. If you've brought me here to—to sack me, well, get it done with, will you?' she finished with a flash of dignity, though her lips quivered.

Without waiting for his reply she turned, groping blindly on the table, but, as her hands closed unsteadily on the envelope, his cold voice arrested her.

'Do credit me with a little intelligence, *mademoiselle*, I implore you. And before you try to protest further, I should perhaps inform you that I have studied the photograph and read the letter. So it would be as well for you to remove that *jeune fille* expression, and admit——'

This time, it was Jenni's turn to interrupt. She snatched up the envelope and cradled it to her, staring at him as angry colour poured into her cheeks.

'How dare you? How dare you read my letter? It's mine, and it's private.' Her voice shook at the thought of anyone—least of all this cold, hostile stranger—fingering her precious possessions. But he merely gave a derisory laugh.

'Oh, come, *chère* Eugénie, we will not prolong this— charade any longer. I was not, as you would say, born yesterday. I repeat, I have seen the photograph, read the letter, as I was doubtless intended to, right from the beginning. I really must congratulate you on your acting abilities. You are obviously wasted in a campsite office.' His voice was dry. 'You have given a performance which Sarah Bernhardt would have been proud of. But the game is over now.'

'What game?' Jenni stared at him, almost dazed by his tirade. Had he gone mad, or had she? Then, as the full meaning of his words sank in, she gave a gasp and the letter dropped unheeded back on to the table.

'What do you mean—you read the letter as you were intended? You surely can't be saying—oh, it's so ridiculous—I can't believe it—that I intended my bag to be brought here to you.' She laughed, an edge of hysteria crackling in her voice.

He shrugged. 'Is it so impossible? I think not. Your bag was found, as I said, in a culvert by the side of the road—its contents spread around it, your so private——' he shot her an unpleasant look '—belongings conveniently beside it for ease of identification. The only flaw is that passports today are valuable currency—like the money, it would not have been left——'

'Oh, for heaven's sake,' Jenni shook her head impatiently, 'you'll be telling me next I arranged to be mugged!'

'Ah, but I only have your—word,' he sneered openly, 'that you were.'

A furious retort burned on her lips. All she had to do was pull aside the neckline of her T-shirt to reveal the still livid bruise on her shoulder, but pride held her back. If he was so determined not to believe her, she would not demean herself by offering physical proof—and, in any case, she shuddered inwardly at the thought of exposing the smallest part of her body to his uncaring gaze.

'Well, believe me or not, it's true. And as for the passport, well, they were kids, not international criminals. The only thing they were interested in was my money.'

She stopped abruptly, biting her lip hard to keep back a sob. Since Raoul had gone away, she had thought of him ceaselessly, the image of his face obscuring her work. But now the joy, the elation she had first felt at Claudette's words had changed into this tight, leaden pain about her ribs. And she still did not know what heinous crime she had committed.

'Sit down.'

Raoul spoke quite softly, yet she flinched at the curt command. Beside him the dog whimpered softly and thrust his nose at Raoul's hand, but he gently pushed the animal away. Behind him, Jenni saw her own distraught reflection in the gilt-framed mirror, and the naked fear on her face awoke a spark of anger in her.

'No, I won't.' She snatched up her bag. 'I'm going.'

But then she hesitated as Raoul repeated his command, the menace in his tone unmistakable. 'You will leave this room when I have finished with you. Now sit.'

He gestured her towards a chair and Jenni gazed at him, as though taking his measure. It was all nonsene, of course. He couldn't possibly force her to stay a moment longer than she wanted. She would defy him and walk out, and slam the door hard behind her . . . She caught his eyes, steely-grey, watching her as though daring her to disobey; she calculated the distance to the door and abandoned all thought of red-blooded defiance. She dropped into the chair, from where she scowled mutinously up at him.

'Now, enough of this folly. What was your father's name?'

Jenni gaped at him, closing her hands into each other to

still their nervous start. Whatever she had expected, it was not this. Deep down, past the fear and bewilderment, a slow pulse of hostility began to beat in her.

'What is that to do with you?'

'Oh, come, *mademoiselle*, we can do better than that. Your father was Philippe Henri Kerouac?'

'Yes,' she replied, through stiff lips, then added stubbornly, 'but it's nothing to do with——'

'So you admit it? You admit that you came here knowing that you were Eugénie Aimée Kerouac?'

She shrugged wearily. 'But you see, I'm not. When Mum—my mother—remarried, my name was changed to Green. Jenni Green,' she added coldly.

But he ignored the challenge in her tone. 'At the time, it would doubtless have seemed a clever idea—an attempt to ingratiate themselves.' He seemed almost to be musing to himself, yet the look he gave her was unequivocally hostile. 'Perhaps it was your mother's idea to name the child after its French grandmother.'

Grandmother? Jenni's mind, still reeling from the verbal onslaught he had subjected her to, struggled feebly to come to grips with the meaning hidden behind his words. She knew that he was being deliberately insulting, that she should leap up in righteous indignation to defend her mother—but from what?

'And that letter,' he gestured towards it, 'it was, of course, the last he wrote to your mother.'

'Yes. He wrote it just before the accident and——' she broke off abruptly, her eyes darkening '—but how did you know that?'

His lips twisted. 'How should I not know, considering that he was coming here, to Les Forêts—to this house? But of course you are well aware of that, are you not, *ma chère?*

As equally you are aware that Philippe was my adoptive brother—and that I, too, bear the name Kerouac!'

CHAPTER FOUR

RAOUL'S voice was savage, but Jenni was scarcely aware of it. She could hardly breathe, yet she was taking in great gulps of air, until her pulses seemed to be echoing inside her brain. She clutched her hands until her nails dug into her palms, and pushed herself hard against the chair, seeking comfort, reassurance even, in the upholstered solidity of its tapestry back.

The room had become strangely hot, she thought in a detached kind of way, for there was no fire and the tall windows at the far end of the room were open. She put her hand up to her forehead to brush away beads of sweat, and tried to stand up. She heard Raoul give an impatient exclamation, then through almost closed eyelids saw him coming towards her, a dark silhouette against the light. Strong hands were pushing her down against the chair, then a glass was thrust unceremoniously to her lips, clinking against her teeth, and she choked as a gulp of scorching liquid went down.

She opened her eyes and, with a pathetic attempt at dignity, gestured him away. 'Th—thank you. I'm all right now. The room was rather hot.'

He set down the glass beside her and regarded her, stony-faced.

'I really must congratulate you. The theatre has lost a quite remarkable young talent. Such a guileless face,' he put a finger under her chin and wrenched her face up towards him, 'and such wide, innocent eyes.'

51

He held her gaze, his eyes scorching, until hers filled with tears. Then, with a contemptuous gesture, he dropped his hand and moved away from her.

Jenni, her fingers picking restlessly at the tapestry chair arms, stared past him through a shimmer of tears at the ornate brass and marble clock on the mantelpiece. Unbelievable though it was, ten minutes, just ten minutes had elapsed since she had come into this room, eager to see Raoul again; now her mind had been numbed, even stupefied, by his cruelty. But the fumes were dissipating from her brain, and now it was working in overdrive.

How ironic it all was! Armed with only the name of a village at the head of a hastily scrawled note, she had come as though on a pilgrimage in search of her father's family, and had found it, not in the village, but here, in the château of Les Forêts. And that he, Raoul, 'Monsieur Raoul . . .' If only, during the past week, one single person had added a surname to that title to which she had become so accustomed, a horrified realisation would have come and she could have fled—appalled, but her cloak of anonymity secure . . .

Raoul's cold voice cut into her thoughts. 'But I am very much afraid, *mademoiselle*, that I was not taken in by the idea of a poor young girl wandering quite by chance up to the gates of her ancestral home. No—the age of fairy-tales is long since dead. So now—to business. I shall telephone François David, the estate lawyer, tomorrow morning. He will have to be told before anyone else.'

'Told? What will he have to be told?' Apprehension made Jenni's voice crack uncertainly.

'Why, that another Eugénie Aimée Kerouac has arrived at Les Forêts. What else?'

From somewhere deep inside Jenni, a hysterical laugh

welled up, but she forced it down. This was no occasion for
weakness; she must remain clear-headed, and escape now,
while there was still time. She sprang to her feet.

'Look. I'm sorry to have upset you. I mean——' Then,
seeing the derisive twist of his lips, she added, 'Please
believe me. It must have been a terrible shock for you
but—don't worry,' there was a faintly bitter inflexion in the
last words, and she set her head proudly, 'I shall leave Les
Forêts tomorrow.'

'Determined to play the part to the end, eh, *ma petite?*'
Raoul's voice was sharp with sarcasm. 'Please, I beg you, no
more dramatic scenes. I have told you what you doubtless
wish to hear. I shall inform our lawyer——'

'No!' The word came out almost as a shout, and Jenni
took an involuntary step towards him. 'You don't understand—you really don't! Yes, it's true I came to Brittany to
find out about my father's past, but if you think——' She
stopped, fumbling desperately for the words. 'If you believe
that I want anything—anything to do with the family who
disowned him when he dared to fall in love with an English
girl, and who caused his death, when he was coming to
plead with them to accept his wife and baby, you're utterly,
totally——' She broke off again, struggling to restrain the
passionate words, then went on a shade more calmly, 'You
really shouldn't have gone snooping through my things,
Monsieur Raoul.' And she had the satisfaction of seeing his
face darken angrily.

As they stared at each other, the hostility between them
almost palpable, the phone began to ring stridently in
another room, so that they both started violently at the
sudden shattering of the tension. Raoul, with an
exclamation of impatience, strode towards a door at the far
end of the room, the dog following close behind. He

wrenched open the door, paused a moment, then said over
his shoulder to Jenni, 'Stay here.' The door closed behind
them.

Think! She must think quickly. She thrust her hands to
her throbbing temples. Get away. Yes, that was it—she
must get away before Raoul returned. For now, and only
now that she was alone, her brain had finally begun to
comprehend the appalling situation into which she had
unwittingly stumbled. Earlier, she had feared to be
dismissed; now, her mind seized on that idea and was
grateful. And she would not even wait for morning—she
would go that instant.

As soon as the idea had occurred to her, she snatched up
her possessions and thrust them into her bag. The passage
was deserted. She sped down it and across the wide hall;
dragging open the heavy front door, she ran two at a time
down the steps to her van. Her trembling fingers were
already turning on the ignition when the door was
wrenched open and Raoul snatched the key from her hand.

'Where do you think you are going?' The fury blazed out
from his face.

'To—to my apartment.' She seemed to have almost lost
the power of speech, the words coming out as a faint croak.

'Not until I have finished with you. Get out!' He gave her
arm a shake.

'N—no. Leave me alone,' she began, but his fingers
tightened round her arm, digging into the tender flesh until
she almost cried out.

'Get out of your own free will, chère Eugénie,' he said
softly, 'or I'll drag you out and hurt you a great deal more in
the process.'

When she still did not at once obey, he gave her arm a
savage jerk, forcing her out of the vehicle. Still keeping his

hold on her, he marched along the front of the château, their footsteps crunching in unison on the gravel as Jenni stumbled along, trying to keep up with his long stride.

She shot a nervous sideways look up at him, and at the sight of his face, set in coldly implacable lines, and his flint-grey eyes, all thoughts of pleading, much less *demanding* that he release her, died.

'Where are you taking me?' she faltered.

'To my private garden—free from prying eyes. We shall continue our conversation there.'

Jenni's stomach tightened in fear. 'But I don't want to.'

'But you see, Eugénie, *I* do.'

They rounded the end of the château and before them was a high stone wall. Without releasing his hold on her, Raoul took a key from a cleft between two stones and unlocked a green-painted wooden door. It swung open, creaking on its hinges, and he thrust her in ahead of him. He closed the door, relocking it from the inside, while Jenni stared about her, momentarily enchanted in spite of herself by the garden.

It was small, bordered on one side by the château, on the other three sides by granite walls whose severe lines were softened by sprawling shrub roses. A series of narrow gravelled paths led between low box hedges to a central granite plinth, surrounded by more roses, and on which was an old, worn sundial. The scene had a cloistered, timeless air of tranquillity about it.

Raoul tugged impatiently at her arm. 'Come.'

He led her to a green metal bench near the sundial, and Jenni, not absolutely in command of her legs, dropped gratefully down on to it. She glanced at her arm, where already a semicircle of angry weals was staining the skin.

'That is nothing to what I would like to do to you.'

Raoul's voice was grim. He was leaning against the stone
plinth, watching her, and after a quick, almost furtive
glance up at him from under her lashes, Jenni's eyes slid
away. For heaven's sake, she told herself impatiently, must
you always turn chicken-yellow at a frown from *Monsieur
Raoul?* Get up—run—climb over the wall. Her eyes swept
around the high, lichened grey walls. No, there was no
escape, and besides, she must be careful, very careful, with
this man. Her first casual impression of him had been truer
than she could possibly have realised. Her glance flickered
back to Raoul. He was watching her, a bleak smile playing
round his lips.

'Yes, the wall is indeed high, and those are my private
apartments, so you can expect no assistance. There is no
escape for you, *ma chère* Eugénie, until I choose.'

'My name isn't——' Jenni began, then she stopped, her
shoulders sagging wearily. Why bother, when he was
impervious to anything she might say? Much better to sit
silent, then this nightmare confrontation would be over the
sooner.

She dragged her eyes from his, and instead let them travel
over the château. An old wistaria had spread almost up to
the level of the grey-tiled roof, its huge mauve flower
racemes hanging heavy against the rosy-pink wall. In the far
corner, a flight of stone steps led up to a narrow walkway,
bounded by low, silver-grey lavender bushes and red roses,
and running beneath the open windows. Raoul's
apartment? Yes, she remembered now that she had been
aware of the delicate scent of roses when she had been
inside.

This beautiful house. Jenni sighed softly. If only her
father, on that final, fatal mission, had succeeded in healing

the rift with his family . . . 'Have faith, *chérie*. When I tell my mother of our little Eugénie, and of the happiness you have both brought me, she will not refuse——'

'Yes, it is indeed a prize worth having, a prize to come far in search of, *n'est-ce pas?*' Raoul's harsh voice shattered her thoughts.

'Please, don't begin again.' She raised her hands placatingly. 'You've read my letter—well, you know that my father wrote it so hurriedly that he scribbled the name of the village, nothing more. My mother refused ever to talk about him, or his family. Yes, it's true!' she exclaimed, when he smiled in patent disbelief. 'And anyway, can I remind you that you yourself directed me—insisted that I came here?'

He shrugged. 'As to that, you were doubtless on your way here, and like a fool I played into your hands. If it is any satisfaction to you, I accept your story of the assault. Even you could not have been so devious, but that does not take away the basic fact. You came, *ma chère*, to give Les Forêts the—what do you call it in English?—the look-over.'

'Once-over,' she replied automatically, her mind still grappling with the implication of his words.

'The once-over. You came, in secret, to examine the estate, to see whether your inheritance would be worth claiming, or——'

'My—inheritance?' Jenni gaped at him in stupefaction, but his expression merely hardened even more.

'I tell you once again—the time for play-acting is at an end. If Les Forêts was revealed as ramshackle, impoverished, as a worthless millstone round your neck, you would have withdrawn, just as silently as you came. The revelation of your identity today has merely hastened matters. You were doubtless biding your time, watchful

for your opportunity, for your astute eyes will have
registered that the estate is very far from being
impoverished.'

Jenni's mind was reeling. Even now, she still could not
take in the full significance of what he was saying.

'Your father showed little interest in the estate, and after
he died——' He lifted his shoulders in a faint, though
expressive, shrug. 'But since I took over the management,
well——' his hands swept around '—it has become as you
see it. But now I find that I have worked body and soul for
twelve years for a——'

'No!' Jenni burst out impetuously, then took a deep,
steadying breath to calm her rising emotion 'Look,' she
began again, her tone more placatory, 'let's be reasonable.
Crazy as the whole idea is, you think that I've turned up
like some black sheep to—to try to steal the estate from you,
don't you?'

She looked at him, but then, as he remained silent, she
went on, 'Well, you can believe me or not when I deny it.
That's your privilege,' she added proudly, 'but anyway,
you needn't worry. I'm leaving, and——'

'Is the idea so crazy? And as for leaving, you do not
seriously expect me to believe that having read the
advertisements in the English newspapers——'

'What advertisements?'

Raoul favoured her with a sneering smile. 'You know
quite well, *ma chère*. The notices inserted by our lawyer, to
comply with the terms of your grandmother's will, asking
for Eugénie Aimée Kerouac to come forward.'

'Sorry to disappoint you, but you see, I never had time to
read the papers,' Jenni retorted, remembering the long,
tiring hours in the hotel when she had often been too
exhausted to do other than crawl off to bed.

'Oh, please!' Raoul held up his hand. 'Having carefully manipulated the whole affair—and what good fortune it must have seemed to you when I actually offered you employment here——' there was a scourging bitterness in his voice that made her wince '—it is unthinkable that you would give up your rights. Oh no, Mademoiselle *Green*, you will get what you have aimed for from the start.'

'I don't understand you.' Jenni was utterly bemused. 'You are the owner of Les Forêts, and you run the estate wonderfully—as people never tire of telling me. So even if I wanted to steal the estate——'

'You say you do not understand,' he interrupted her, the barely contained impatience snapping in his voice. 'Very well, I shall explain the situation—in words of one half of a syllable. You know quite well that I am an adopted son—legally, it is true, and my name was changed to Kerouac, but I am adopted none the less——'

'You must listen!' Jenni banged her fists on her knees in frustration. 'I don't want anything to do with the estate, I tell you. Look at me.' She held out her hands expressively. 'I'm English. I don't belong here. I'm not this Eugénie Aimée Kerouac. She—she was someone else, someone who only existed as a baby on a photograph.'

She fumbled blindly in her bag for the faded photograph, glimpsing momentarily the image of the young couple, laughing into each other's eyes as the baby on the girl's lap laughed too, taking her carefree mood from theirs. She held it up to him with a fierce gesture. 'You've seen this. I found it—together with the letter, after my mother died. They were hidden in a drawer, tied up with red ribbon.' Her voice trembled, but then she forced herself to go on.

'Well, I never saw my mother like this—smiling, happy,

loving, I mean. So, if you think I want anything to do with
the family, or the place that did that to her——' She broke
off, biting her lip, then went on, her voice bitter, 'I'm Jenni
Green. I've got my passport back. I'm leaving in the
morning, and you can forget that I ever came.'

'No!' he said sharply. 'You miss, by luck or intention, the
most crucial part of all. Let you leave? Even if I were fool
enough to believe you, do you think I would permit you to
go, to be aware all the time, as of a bomb ticking away, that
any time you wished to return, you could wrest half of the
estate from me?'

'Half the estate?' Jenni gaped.

'So you are not leaving, simply because I want you here,
where I can keep you under scrutiny.'

She shook her head in a vain attempt to clear it. 'D—do
you mean that my gr—my father's mother, left half the
estate to me?'

He nodded. 'A deathbed change of heart.' His lips
twisted. 'Though after this lapse of time, I had convinced
myself that the child was a mere figment of Philippe's
imagination, to be flung at his mother when he stormed
out. But now,' he gave her a grim smile, 'you are here.'

'Well, let me go then,' she repeated, almost abstractedly.
How ironic it all was, she thought. At last, her chance to
feel at home, really belong somewhere—to someone, for if
her grandmother had not died, she would surely have
welcomed her, or at least tolerated her, as her son's child.

Raoul shook his head. 'It is too late. In a place like this,
rumour abounds. Yes,' he went on quickly, as though to
keep pace with his racing thoughts, 'it is not unlikely that
the *gendarme* who brought me your possessions had himself
read the letter and realised the implications for me. No,
temporarily at least, my hands are tied. You have defeated

me, I admit it.'

'But I'm not trying to defeat you,' said Jenni heavily. 'I don't want to fight you.' In fact, all she *did* want to do was crawl away and nurse the smarting lacerations that his words had inflicted on her.

'And besides,' he continued, as though not even hearing her, 'there is the will. I owe too much to my adoptive mother to thwart her dying wishes. And so I promise you that, contrary to my own personal desires, if for whatever devious motive you should try to leave Les Forêts, I shall hunt you down and bring you back, by force if necessary.'

'I—I see,' she said slowly. 'Well, thanks for the warning,' she added, with a shaky attempt at levity. She was baffled, even frightened, by the arrogant self-assurance of this man. 'I shall hunt you down.' And he would too, she knew with a sick lurch of fear—and show her no mercy when he found her . . .

Her whole body felt weak, and a dull, grey lethargy was creeping stealthily through her veins. It must be the shock, she thought with an almost detached clarity; one hammer blow after another. Somehow, she forced herself to stand.

'I won't listen to any more,' she said. 'I'm going back to my apartment now.'

She heard the pathos in her voice, and to her horror felt hot tears burning her eyes. She turned away quickly and, thrusting her hands into her jeans' pockets, walked off quickly, fearful lest he try to prevent her. However, he only followed her to the door in silence. While he unlocked it, she toyed absently with one of the large creamy-white blooms on a rosebush beside her, and bent to sniff its honeyed centre.

'It was first cultivated on the estate three centuries ago.'

Raoul spoke just behind her. 'It was named for one of your ancestors, Isabelle de Kerouac. Her portrait is in the château. You will see that the centre of each flower is dark crimson; the local people used to say that there was a drop of her heart's blood in every rosebud.'

She carefully folded back the centre petals to reveal the tiny, dusky-red blotch, as Raoul went on, his voice conversational, 'She and her lover poisoned her husband. They were burned to death in the village square.'

Jenni gave a sudden exclamation of pain and looked down at the gout of blood which was oozing from her finger, where one of the savagely barbed thorns had ripped the flesh.

Then, as he relocked the door behind them and pushed the key into its niche, she turned away from his mocking smile, clapped her hand to her mouth to stifle a sob, and fled . . .

CHAPTER FIVE

. . . SHE was running on leaden legs, down an endless avenue of grotesquely shaped yew trees, where at every twisting turn she was confronted by a darkly menacing shape, which resolved itself over and over again into Raoul Kerouac . . .

Jenni woke with a shudder of terror. Her eyes flew open, then she screwed them up against the brilliant light which poured in through the open shutters—overlooked in her frantic haste the previous night.

She had stumbled up the steps into her apartment, locking the door behind her with shaking hands, then flung herself down on the narrow bed. Why had she come to this place? Why had she not been content to remain in England, where, had she but known it, she was secure, able to handle her life? Now, the world was shaking itself out around her ears, while Raoul despised her as a liar, an unwanted intruder . . .

She rolled on to her back and stared up at the ceiling with dull eyes. Suppose she were to pinch herself very hard; could she possibly make the previous evening's traumatic happenings into an illusion, something no more real than the terrifying nightmare she had just escaped from? It was almost as though, she thought with bewilderment, she had stepped, like Alice, out of her ordinary Jenni Green existence, into some contorted looking-glass world where nothing, she knew with heart-stopping certainty, could ever again be quite the same . . .

Her mouth was parched. She hauled herself up on the pillow and reached for the tumbler, half-full on the cabinet beside her bed. The water was stale, but she greedily gulped some down, then cradled the glass in her hands, one finger encircling the rim as she stared at the opposite wall. Alice had stepped back through the mirror, to find the reassuring comfort of familiar things—a playroom, a cat, a clock; surely even for Jenni it need not be too late. Perhaps Raoul's threat had been idle bluff. Could he possibly find her in England, and would he really want to anyway?

As she set down the glass, she caught sight of her watch and gave a gasp of horror. Nine-thirty! She should have been in the office since eight. She threw back the sheet and leaped out of bed, faint wisps of terror from the nightmare still clinging tenaciously to her mind. But then she stood, chewing her bottom lip anxiously, her thoughts still in utter turmoil. Whatever should she do? After the scene the previous night, her whole being shrank from the mere idea of coming face to face with Raoul again. She could flee, as every instinct was telling her to, but there would be no safe haven for her, even if she managed to reach the far side of the Channel, which was doubtful. She would live in constant fear of his running her to earth and forcing her to return, as his prisoner if need be, as he had threatened.

And besides, if she left without warning it would put Claudette, who had been so kind to her, into as much of a state as when Marie-Christine had so thoughtlessly disappeared. So she would, for this morning at least, go to the office and hope that Raoul would have the discretion to keep his distance from her. Now though, late or not, she must have a shower to freshen herself up to face whatever— or rather whoever—was waiting for her on the other side of that door.

She closed the shutters, plunging the room into a welcome twilight, looked out clean bra and pants, jeans and a buttercup yellow T-shirt, and dropped them on to the bed. She hesitated, checked that the door was thoroughly locked, and went through to the shower-room.

She turned the shower on full, so that the cooling water burst in exhilarating, cascading rivulets over her face and body, obliterating everything for a few minutes except her sensuous delight in the feel of the jets playing over her skin. Roughly blotting her body dry, she flicked the towel up into a turban around her streaming hair and went back through to the bedroom.

In the semi-darkness, and still half blinded by the water droplets which formed prisms on her lashes, she fumbled on the bed for her underwear; as she found it, she gave a gasp of pure terror as simultaneously her hand encountered a warm, solid body and another, larger hand closed over her slender wrist. She jerked back, flailing out wildly with her free hand, until that too was trapped in a hard, unyielding grip. There was a short, undignified tussle among the folds of the duvet, silent except for Jenni's panting breath, then she was lying ignominiously on her back, imprisoned by a heavy arm, her wrists still pinioned, so that the more she struggled the more the soft skin was twisted painfully, until at length she lay still.

'That is much better.'

Raoul's voice was in her ear, and at the overt mockery in it helpless rage kindled inside her and she braced her body to spring from his grasp. But his hold tightened on her remorselessly, until a little grunt of pain was forced from her.

'Please—you're hurting me,' she whispered, and his hands slightly slackened their grip.

Only then did the full realisation sink in—that she was quite naked under his grasp. She swallowed, grateful for the twilight gloom to hide the intense blush which was bursting out all over her body.

'L-let me get dressed, please.' Her voice shook slightly.

'Be sensible, then.' There was an unspoken warning in his voice and he lifted his hand in a slight gesture of release, allowing her to roll away from him, off the bed.

Ignoring her underwear, Jenni reached for her jeans and T-shirt and, her back turned to him, somehow dragged them on.

Her eyes had become used to the dim, almost subterranean light, which filtered in through the gap in the shutters, so that she could now, for the first time, see Raoul clearly. He sprawled, every bit as dark and menacing as he had been in her dream, and quite at ease, on her bed. He was watching her, his face all hard planes in the shadow cast by the crook of his arm, his moody grey eyes intent on her, disturbing, undermining her. Why had he forced his way in, intruding on even this tiny island of privacy? After the dreadful scene between them last night, how could he have been so insensitive as to thrust himself on her like this? She took refuge in anger.

'How did you get in here? I locked the door, I know I——Oh!' She stopped suddenly, biting her lip. So she had not imagined that small, secret smile as Raoul had slipped that other key into his pocket. She smiled grimly to herself. She had certainly been right to feel a distinct unease about his ease of access to her apartment, even though, since that first day, she had managed to dismiss it from her mind.

'Well, now you're here, you can just leave again,' she snapped, and with a vague idea of imposing some slight inhibition on his behaviour by throwing the door wide open, she put her hand on the doorknob. She wrenched at it angrily when it would not open, then rounded on him, all caution forgotten.

'You—you've stolen my key. Just give it back, will you?' she stormed.

He held up a hand in protest. 'Oh, not stolen, *ma chère*—merely borrowed.'

The drawl of devilment in his voice infuriated her. How dared he come sauntering in as though he owned not only the apartment, but herself as well? She itched to leap at him, attack him physically, but then the warning in his eyes brought her up sharply. No imprudent behaviour. She took a long breath, then said very distinctly, 'This is my apartment, and would you—please—leave now?'

'When I have spoken to you. Now,' he patted the bed beside him, 'sit down.'

His tone, though, was mild and for the first time Jenni looked at him closely, her eyes narrowing with distrust. The previous night he had been tense, angry, stalking about the room as though incapable of stillness, throwing himself first into a chair, then leaning against the mantelpiece. Now—her perceptions registered the fact with acute apprehension—he was relaxed, almost faintly amused by the whole situation, as though—she swallowed hard—as though he had reached some firm decision.

Without a word, she sat down rather suddenly on the extreme edge of the bed, contenting herself with saying acidly, 'I hope it won't take long. I have a lot to do and it's my free afternoon. I'm—I'm going to the beach,' she added, on the spur of the moment.

'Alone?'

Alerted by something—a sharpness—in his voice, Jenni swung round, but his face was unreadable.

'What do you mean—alone?'

'I am quite sure you know exactly what I mean. Were you intending to go with that English camper with whom you were flirting so outrageously before I went away?'

His voice was cool with distaste, and it set her teeth on edge. Flirting? Outrageously? True, Alan had dropped into the office many times during the week—had spent quite a time there only the previous afternoon, when they had laughed a lot together, but—her lips tightened as a slow surge of anger built inside her.

'You——' she began, and raised her hand to strike him, but quick as thought Raoul seized her uplifted arm and they stared into each other's eyes.

'How dare you say that?' she gasped. 'He—he was asking me if we had any freebie leaflets—free, to you,' she added, as his brows went up coldly, 'about the stone rows at Carnac. It took me rather a long time to find them, that's all.'

'Really?' The disbelief was patent in his voice and it inflamed her anger still more, so that she rushed on injudiciously.

'He—he's an archaeological student, you see, and very hard up, but you wouldn't understand about anything like that, would you?'

He had destroyed a pleasant friendship. She would never again be able to wholly meet Alan's frank, brown-eyed regard. And what was more, she suddenly knew with overwhelming certainty that Raoul had done it with cold deliberation. But why?

He shook her arm impatiently. 'You still have not answered my question. Are you going——?'

'No, I'm not. I'm going on my own. Not that it's anything in the least to do with you if I go alone or if I choose to go with the whole——'

'Do not be absurd,' he broke in. 'You must know quite well that in your new position, whether you wish it or not, your way of conducting yourself must be different. More, not less, is demanded of you, and you will not, of course, be permitted to form relationships with the campers.'

'Oh, for heaven's sake!' He was surely being ridiculous, and yet somehow the word ridiculous was not easily applied to this man. And besides, she knew him well enough by now to sense that there was method in all that he did. Nevertheless, she was not able to bite back her retort. 'What a stupid fuss about nothing! And I don't need you to tell me how to behave——'

At the flash of anger in his eyes she broke off in alarm, tensing herself, too late, to leap back out of reach. He seized her by the arms and dragged her roughly across the bed towards him, disregarding her futile struggles.

'You've said enough. Be quiet!'

When she tried to jerk back away from him, one hand effortlessly cupped her head, his fingers outspread in her hair, so that she was imprisoned against him. She sprawled helplessly across his body, her upraised hands trapped against the fine cotton of his shirt, feeling the twin drumbeat of their hearts. She must fight him, but it was almost impossible. She was being drawn down, slowly, inexorably, to drown in a strange, dark, bottomless whirlpool . . .

She felt Raoul slide his other hand behind her back, impatiently dragging the T-shirt from the waistband of her jeans, then brushing lightly, yet somehow possessively, across the bare flesh of her spine. Darting pinpricks of electricity followed the trail of his fingers across her skin, then as his fingertips circled unhurriedly up her back she gave an incoherent murmur and closed her eyes. The scent of his spicy aftershave, of his warm body, was everywhere, surrounding her, permeating her whole being. She leaned against him and gave a tiny sigh of pleasure, just as Raoul loosened his grip on her and, holding her by the elbows, pushed her away from him.

Dazed, she put out a hand to steady herself on the bed and stared blankly at him, almost unable at first to take in what he was saying.

'So, now we have settled that little dispute. It *is* my right to tell you how to behave when appropriate, and I am warning you now not to be tempted to indulge in a relationship with any of the young campers.'

Settled that little dispute! So that had been the sole purpose of the embrace which had left her dizzy and trembling. She gave an outraged gasp and leaped off the bed.

'Will you please go now? I'm already late for work, so——'

'Yes, you are—very late.'

Raoul ostentatiously looked at his watch and she shot him a smouldering look. How could he? He knew quite well why she had overslept and was wan and heavy-eyed this morning. Still, she would not allow herself to rise to his bait.

'However, you are most fortunate.' That hateful, ironic note again. 'The office has not, after all, been left unattended for the last two hours.'

Poor Claudette, Jenni thought involuntarily; another terror session with the computer.

'Yes,' Raoul went on ruminatively, 'it is indeed lucky that Marie-Christine was able to make up for your deficiency.'

'Marie-Christine?' Jenni's jaw sagged. 'But—but she's

left.'

He laughed shortly. 'Alas, no. She arrived on my doorstep at seven this morning, under the close escort of both her parents, subdued, pink-eyed, chastened if not chaste, and touchingly desirous of returning here to work. She is in the office now.'

'I—see,' Jenni said slowly. 'And what about me, then?'

Raoul raised his shoulders in an elegant, Gallic shrug, and spread his hands expressively. 'As to that, well, we shall just have to see, *n'est-ce pas, ma chère?*' And she thought suddenly, you devil, you've really enjoyed telling me, haven't you?

'You said something?' Raoul's eyes glinted and she set her chin proudly.

'Nothing.' Then she added, stiff-lipped, 'Tell me, hasn't any woman ever kicked you in the teeth? I'm sure a good many must have really longed to.'

He showed those white teeth for an instant, then, 'No, and I am quite certain that no woman would ever be—foolish enough to try.'

He uncoiled himself from the bed. 'And now, I have to go out on estate business for the day, and as, willing or not, I now appear to have a new partner, you will come too.'

Come too—on a day-long trip with Raoul? Although his demeanour was so very different today, the mere thought still filled her with something very like terror.

'If you think I'm coming out with you, after the way you tr-treated me last night——' There was a tremor in her voice and she broke off as, for a moment, she relived that searing confrontation. But Raoul, as though oblivious of the effect the scene between them must have had on her, heaved a sigh and cast his eyes ceilingwards.

'Why is it that everyone else obeys me without demur,

whereas with you it is always *no, no, no?* It is imperative that you accompany me. As I said, I am going on estate business, and you must begin to learn something of your—unexpected inheritance.'

There was an underlying bite to his last words, and Jenni stared at him mutinously for a few moments but said nothing.

'And now,' he continued smoothly, 'you are not coming with me dressed like that, so you had better get changed.'

'I'm dressed already, and I'm not changing. That's if I do agree to come with you,' she added truculently.

'But I am not accustomed to escorting young women who——' his eyes flicked up and down her body '—display their not inconsiderable charms so blatantly.'

Ignoring her gasp of outrage, he looked down at his watch again. 'I shall wait below for you. You have ten minutes.'

She scowled at him as he dug out the key from the pocket of his pale blue denims. Huh, so it was all right for him to wear skin-tight jeans, she thought sourly. For a long moment their eyes locked in silent combat, then he turned away.

The door closed and his quick footsteps clattered down the steps. Jenni leaned her heated face against the cold mirror of the wardrobe, closed her eyes and whispered fervently, 'I hate you, Raoul Kerouac. Oh, how I hate you!'

She moved back and regarded herself in the narrow line of mirror. He had been right, of course. Was he ever wrong? she thought with a dying flicker of fury. Claudette had let her use the kitchen washing maching the previous afternoon, and she must have set the water too hot; overnight, her clothes had somehow lost a size. Now, the jeans strained across her flat stomach and the slender curves of her hips, while the thin yellow cotton of the T-shirt clung to the high, taut outline of her breasts, surely as never before. She coloured involuntarily. Oh, damn him! No other man had ever succeeded in making her feel uncomfortably aware of her own body in quite this way before . . .

What had he said—ten minutes? And no doubt if she were a second late he would be back up the steps to carry her bodily down to the car.

She ripped the clothes off, replacing them with the first dress she came to—a pretty, mauve smock in soft cotton. Her hair was still damp, so she dragged it impatiently into a huge knot on her neck in an attempt to make the contours of her face looked older, less girlish, then wriggled her feet into white, high-heeled sandals. She snatched up her bag, stood still for a moment to get her breath, then sauntered, deliberately sedate, down the steps.

Raoul was squatting on his haunches, watching the peacocks. He straightened up slowly as she approached, and some devilment made her hold up her arms and twirl lightly in front of him, as she said in mock submission, 'I hope you approve, my lord?'

He subjected her to a long scrutiny, but merely said gravely, 'A distinct improvement.'

As he opened the car door for her, she toyed briefly with the idea of informing him that the dress, like many of her clothes, had come from the excellent charity shop near the hotel where she had worked, but then decided against it; it might, she thought reluctantly, prove altogether too much for a fastidious nature to be sharing the heirship—was that the word?—with a psychedelic van *and* charity-shop clothes.

As Raoul swung himself in beside her, his hips brushed casually against hers, momentarily trapping her dress, so that Jenni, the fine hairs on her skin set tingling by the

unnerving sensation of his nearness, edged furtively away.
Raoul, though, was apparently quite unconcerned by their
proximity, and unaware of her reaction for, without another
word, he switched on the engine and the Citroën leaped
into life, scattering outraged peacocks before it.

Their route took them past the back of the château,
leaving a small lake with a boathouse to their left. Beyond
was a sweep of rolling, broadleaved woodland, and Raoul
gestured towards it.

'That is what gave Les Forêts its name, although it was
much larger centuries ago—it was a royal forest, and the
house a royal hunting lodge.'

In spite of her wish to appear utterly careless of anything
at all to do with the Kerouac inheritance, Raoul's words
were irresistible. She gazed out, seeing in her mind's eye a
hunting party, the women in furs and velvet habits which
swept the ground. Perhaps Isabelle de Kerouac had
galloped through those wide, cathedral-like aisles among
the beech trees.

'One of the Kerouac ladies found favour with Louis the
Fourteenth, and as a result the family was ennobled, though
after the Revolution the estate passed to a *cadet* branch of
the family and then it was plain Kerouac again.'

They had left the woods behind now and were driving
past ring-fenced fields, lush meadows and a prosperous-
looking farmhouse. Jenni sat silent as a wave of unexpected
emotion broke over her. Here, her father had grown up: run
through those meadows, maybe paddled a boat on the dark
waters of the lake—although perhaps not. Madame
Kerouac, she felt certain, had been a smothering, over-
protective mother. No, no boat. Perhaps, instead, he had
ridden a pony, as that little boy was perched astride that
ancient cart-horse over there . . . She would be glad when

they had left Les Forêts behind. Here, far from the bland, characterless campsite, the past was pressing potently in on her. Which was no doubt precisely why Raoul had chosen to come this way, she thought resentfully, and turned her head away.

Just as he slowed to turn out into the road, though, she caught sight of a small house, built not in the local Breton style, but of the same pinkish stone and soft grey-blue tiles as the château, and almost surrounded by trees and shrubbery.

'What a lovely house!' she exclaimed.

'The former lodge-keeper's cottage,' Raoul informed her briefly, seemingly too occupied in turning into the busy stream of traffic to spare the cottage even a cursory glance.

'Does anyone live there now?'

'Oh, off and on—mainly off.'

An unsatisfactory reply but, looking at the hard outline of Raoul's face, Jenni knew that she would get no other.

As she craned for a last glimpse of the cottage, Raoul asked, 'Are you not interested in where I am taking you?'

She gave a faint grimace. 'Oh, I'm sure you'll tell me when you're ready.'

'There is no secret, *ma chère*. I have an appointment with our fisheries agent in Concarneau. It will be an ideal means for you to learn something of our *affaires*, and be introduced to some more of our employees.'

'Oh.'

Our *affaires!* Our employees! To cover her uncertainty, Jenni made great play of tucking in her swirling skirt firmly against her legs, and folded her hands primly in her lap. She simply could not work out what was going through Raoul's head. All his furious anger of the previous night—and she could understand, even sympathise with it—had vanished.

She would, she thought nervously, have expected, after a
long night in which to contemplate and at length fully
comprehend the blow which had struck him, that he would
now have been even angrier. And yet today he was quite
different, seemingly accepting the situation they both found
themselves in. She shook her head slightly. It was all very
puzzling, and she felt again the uneasiness she had
experienced in her apartment, the fear that Raoul had come
to a decision, and that somehow that decision would all too
closely involve her.

In the meantime, the attractive Breton countryside was
flashing past: small villages, stone churches, solid-looking
farmsteads, surrounded by fields lined with neat rows of
leeks and lettuces. She would not freely have chosen to
come, but somehow, in spite of her tensions, she would try
to enjoy this day. She sat back in her seat more comfortably.

'Very wise. Yes, I too think today is to be enjoyed.'

Jenni started at his words, and though he did not look at
her, she saw his mouth quirk with amusement. He had, it
seemed, a disconcerting ability to read her thoughts at will.
She turned her head away quickly, thinking that she must
guard not simply her tongue, but her very mind. Perhaps it
was that, although he had been brought close to the heart of
the Kerouac family, while she, through her father's
estrangement, had drifted to the periphery, underneath,
maybe—maybe they shared a family closeness. Jenni
swallowed nervously. She hoped not. There were more than
enough complications in their relationship already!

CHAPTER SIX

IMPERATIVE? That was what Raoul had said when he'd insisted that she accompany him on this trip. But was her presence really so vital? reflected Jenni, as she sat in the agent's office. Suppressing a slight shudder at its raw fierceness, she sipped the cognac that Monsieur Vauquet had pressed on her, and sat, a silent observer of the conversation between him and Raoul. And come to that, from what she could understand of their rapid-fire discussion, the *'affaires'* could just as easily have been dealt with by a single telephone call. But no doubt, she thought, Raoul liked to keep his hand firmly on the tiller, to place the personal stamp of his authority on all matters relating to the estate.

This seemed to be confirmed when he steered her across the quay towards a group of tough-looking, denim-clad fishermen.

'Now, come and meet Jean-Jacques and some of his crew.'

The men greeted her respectfully, though with no obsequiousness, and Jenni found herself, after the first nervousness, beginning to relax under the uncomplicated scrutiny of their keen yet friendly eyes. One addressed her as Mademoiselle Kerouac, and she opened her mouth to correct his mistake, then thought, it's too complicated to explain, and what does it matter, anyway?

Polite exchanges over, she backed off a little, leaving Raoul deep in a conversation with them which she could not hope to follow, for they had lapsed into what she supposed must be Breton dialect. She watched them from behind her sunglasses. Raoul, though head and shoulders taller than the rest, shared, it occurred to her all at once, their hard, even flinty toughness. He was totally at ease with them—even down to some back-slapping jokes and much laughter—and yet she could not help but be keenly aware of the very obvious respect with which they deferred to his words.

From the quay, they walked across the causeway to the *ville fortifiée*, the ancient walled town, and strolled for a while round the narrow cobbled streets with their lovingly restored houses and shops. In one, she bought a pretty Breton-ware bowl, with 'Suzanne' painted on it—the nearest she could find to 'Sue'. Raoul showed no reaction when she explained the reason for her choice, but as she put it in her bag she suddenly wondered when she would see her stepsister again.

She recalled the impression she'd had earlier that Raoul had come to some decision about her. He had presumably decided that the present situation was untenable, but, though he was clearly as hard as the granite rock of Brittany, she felt instinctively that he was no crook. However unwelcome her existence might be, he would not cheat her or attempt to renege on her grandmother's wishes. She chewed her lip reflectively. Perhaps he'd decided to offer her an allowance—a fair pay-off for her share of the estate, plus a ferry ticket, one-way, of course, back to England. That would be by far the best solution for both of them, she told herself resolutely.

But in that case, why was he bothering to go through the motions of introducing her to the estate's affairs? Once again, she gave up the struggle. Raoul might have that disconcerting knack of seeing into her thoughts, but she was finding it impossible to read his mind. To avoid yet another of his searching glances, for he was right beside her, she plunged into another shop . . .

They ate dinner in a small country *auberge*, then soon after turned off the busy highway into a narrow side road which Raoul informed her was a quieter route back to Les Forêts. Unaccountably, at his words, Jenni found herself wanting to shout out, but I don't want to get back!

She forced the words down, but it was true. She dreaded getting back to Les Forêts. From the moment they had arrived in Concarneau Raoul had been a relaxed, charming companion, and she too had gradually unwound, and had even, as she'd hoped, enjoyed the day. It was almost as if there had been an unspoken truce between them, but tonight—tonight, they would be back on their former battleground . . .

The sports car—English, as Raoul later pointed out—veered round the sharp bend at horrifying speed, and though at the last minute the driver somehow straightened up and flashed past, Raoul, in taking evasive action, was forced up against the low stone wall. He got out, angrily surveyed the front of the car, raised the bonnet, and gave vent to a torrent of pungent language, in which 'les Anglais' featured prominently.

Jenni slid across the seat and scrambled out on his side. Through the dusk, she could see a large dent in the front bumper, but otherwise, she thought with a surge of relief, the damage seemed minimal.

'The car cannot be moved. We shall have to stay here until morning.'

'Here?'

Her eyes anxiously ranged across the endless line of green

meadows, empty of all life except a few cows standing beside a nearby stone barn.

Raoul gave an impatient exclamation. 'Of course not *here*. There is a farm ahead. They will know of somewhere to stay.'

Jenni surveyed the car again, then began tentatively, 'It doesn't seem too bad to me——'

'The damage is internal,' he replied curtly. 'Remain here, please.'

Jenni gave his retreating back a scowl, then shrugged philosophically. However hard he might try, she simply would not allow his change of mood to spoil the day. As for the night—a qualm ran through her at the thought of spending it in close proximity to him, but then an irrepressible smile broke across her face. After all, Raoul could always do the impossible, and now, she felt sure, he would conjure up from the wilds of Brittany a four-star hotel!

When he returned, he was carrying a small white bundle, and as she eyed it curiously, he said succinctly, 'A nightdress.'

She gaped at him in astonishment. 'For me?'

'Well, not for me, I assure you. Catch.' And he casually tossed it to her.

'But—but where are we going to sleep?'

'There.'

Raoul was locking the car, and merely gestured with his head. Jenni's eyes swivelled towards——

'I don't believe it! We can't sleep in a barn!' she almost wailed. So much for the four-star hotel. It was to be a couple of bales of scratchy hay. And there would be mice—or, she swallowed, even rats, 'I—I think I'll sleep in the car.'

'What an ungrateful young woman you are! *Monsieur* offers you his best barn, and you stand in the middle of the road wringing your hands. Now,' his voice hardened, 'come, unless you wish me to carry you.'

When she still hesitated, he made a determined move towards her, so she walked past him quickly, head in the air. He opened the gate and gestured her past; her high heels sank in the soft, oozing mud—at least, remembering the cows, she only hoped it *was* mud.

There was a rough track to the barn, and Raoul took a firm grip of her hand, as though half afraid she might flee into the soft dusk. She gritted her teeth as she stubbed her toe hard, but a moment later a little cry of pain was forced from her.

'What is the matter now?' Raoul did not sound sympathetic, merely irritable.

'I trod on a thistle.'

'Well, if you will wear such unsuitable shoes . . .'

Jenni swelled like an indignant turkey cock. 'Of all the—I was going to wear flat shoes this morning, but *you* made me——'

'All right.' He held up a hand in mock apology. 'Anyway, we are here now,' he added, quite unnecessarily, as the barn loomed uninvitingly over them.

He unlocked a small door, reached inside, and flicked on a light. So they were not to be in the dark. That was something, at least. When she followed him, however, she saw with amazement, no bales of hay—though somehow the faint, sweet smell of mown grass was in the air—but a large room, furnished with old, over-sized pieces of furniture and colourful rag rugs. Against one wall was an enormous wood-burning stove, its glass door open and a fire neatly laid inside. Beyond a half-door, Jenni's bewildered eyes took in modern pine kitchen units, while up a short flight of open-tread stairs there was another door. She tried to close her mind to the implications of that one single door, but then, as Raoul came towards her, she shivered suddenly.

'You are cold.'

He stooped down and put a match to the fire, as Jenni stood uncertainly.

'But—what is this place?'

'A *gîte*. Tourist accommodation. We are fortunate that it is empty. An English family will arrive tomorrow, but for tonight Madame says we are welcome to it.'

The fire caught immediately, the kindling crackling into cheerful life, and Raoul pulled the cumbersome, uncomfortable-looking sofa in front of it. He glanced at her.

'Are you hungry? I am sure *Madame* could provide something.'

'Oh, no, really,' she said stiffly, then added, 'Thank you.'

She perched on the hard sofa, feeling decidedly ill at ease. The camaraderie they had apparently shared that afternoon had vanished completely now, and she felt awkward, even nervous, in this confined, intimate situation with him. Raoul, though, she thought resentfully, was quite at his ease as usual.

He dropped casually on to the floor beside her, leaning against the sofa, his hands out towards the flames. His shoulder was against her knee, his head inches from her hand, so that if she only moved it a little, she could bury her fingers in that thick, dark thatch of hair, and——

She gulped, as every muscle in her tensed. Raoul must have felt the sudden movement, for he turned to look up at her.

'Now, how do you propose that we pass the rest of the evening, until bedtime?'

His eyes were a strange silvery-grey in the dancing light from the fire, and she looked away hastily, fixing her gaze on one enamelled leg of the stove.

'Can you think of anything we might do, Jenni?' His voice was soft and intimate, the 'Jenni' almost a caress, and the hairs on her neck stirred uneasily.

'I—I don't know,' she said lamely, and her voice cracked slightly on the final word.

Quite unable to meet his eyes, her own roamed feverishly around the enormous room, then lighted on a wide recess in the stone hearth.

'Oh, look, jigsaws!' she almost babbled with relief. 'I love doing them.'

In fact, she had not touched one since Sue was small, but the tattered-looking boxes had the desired effect. Raoul laughed and pulled a face.

'Well—toys for visitors' children on rainy days was not perhaps what I had in mind,' he said drily, 'but, *faute de mieux*——'

He gave a rueful shrug, then reached one of the boxes down, tossed it into her lap and carried across a low coffee-table.

She tipped out the pieces in silence, and began stolidly turning over each, as though by this mechanical action she might hold on to some semblance of reality. Raoul, meanwhile, took a lurid-covered paperback from the same recess and settled himself back at her feet, with an air of being about to enjoy himself immensely.

The logs hissed and spurted behind their polished glass door, a shutter rattled softly. The jigsaw was a copy of an Impreesionist painting of a rainswept street, all soft greys and muted blues, and Jenni soon gave up the sofa to crouch on the rag rug, her chin propped on one hand, frowning in concentration. She had almost forgotten about Raoul, behind her, when he threw down his book.

'Ugh! Enough of that rubbish. I will help you.'

Before she could move a muscle, he had plumped himself down at the opposite side of the table and was hard at work on a section of the grey sky. Once, their fingers brushed against each other as they both reached for the same piece, and Jenni's nerve-ends tingled at the touch, but Raoul seemed to have all his attention on the puzzle before him and to be quite oblivious of her.

She stole a look at him. His face, softened by the firelight, looked younger, almost—almost vulnerable, she thought with a strange pang, while under the dark sweep of lashes his normally hard, even calculating eyes had a tender brilliance. His lips, so often compressed into a thin line, were softened into a sensual curve. He brushed back a lock of dark hair which had fallen across his brow, and at the simple gesture her insides seemed to melt in a treacherous, unwanted longing.

Aghast at her reaction, she turned hastily back to the scattered pieces and began almost fiercely ramming them together. As if sensing her confusion, he raised his head to give her a quizzical look, and in an attempt to disguise the reason for her unease she asked, 'Won't they be worried—at Les Forêts, I mean?'

'No. I rang the housekeeper from the farmhouse. I told her that we were unexpectedly delayed, and would return tomorrow.'

'Oh.' Jenni compressed her lips. She could just imagine the raised eyebrows and clacking tongues as this piece of interesting news filtered through the estate. 'Didn't you tell her about the car?'

Raoul laughed easily. 'Oh, don't worry. There is no need to fear for your reputation. Madame Cherbay is very discreet. She has been at Les Forêts as long as I can remember. She was your grandmother's personal maid when I was first brought from the orphanage.'

'The orphanage?' Jenni stared at him. 'But I thought you were a member of the family.'

Raoul hesitated, as if in reluctant response to the question in her voice, then said slowly, 'So I am. My father was a distant cousin of your grandfather, although for years there was no contact between the two families. My parents had always struggled financially, and when I was a baby they decided to try their hand at farming in West Africa.'

He broke off abruptly, but then, as Jenni looked enquiringly, he went on brusquely, 'When I was eight, they were both killed by insurgents, and I was shipped back to an orphanage near Marseilles. One year later, the Kerouacs tracked me down, brought me back to Les Forêts and adopted me as their younger son.'

He glanced at her and, at the expression on her face, his lips twisted. 'Oh, no tears, I beg you. I did not intend to wring your soft heart. It was a long time ago and besides, my year in the orphanage taught me many useful lessons. For example,' he gave her a wry look, 'what I have, I hold on to.'

Jenni gazed at him, seeing for a moment not the tough, self-assured man, but the frightened, bewildered child. However much the adult man might try to shrug it off, how terrible a trauma it must have been for him. And, of course, this explained much of his reaction the previous evening. Although she still flinched at the searing memory, none the less she felt she could now understand, even begin to forgive.

Raoul stretched himself lazily like a giant cat and looked

at his watch. 'Time for bed. You are tired, and I too did not sleep well last night.'

His eyes were perfectly expressionless as he put his hands under her arms to raise her to her feet. But, as he did so, she stumbled over the rug and clutched instinctively at his arm to steady herself. Although he was wearing only a thin, short-sleeved shirt, his flesh under her fingers felt warm. She glanced down fleetingly and saw the tanned skin, the sheen of dark hairs. Somehow, that arm seemed all at once vibrantly, frighteningly alive, and she withdrew her fingers quickly from its contact as though it had scorched her.

He went on ahead of her up the stairs and threw open the door, Jenni trailing unwillingly after him. When she went in, he was sitting on the edge of a huge, old-fashioned brass bedstead which all but filled the room.

'Have you ever slept in a feather bed before, Jenni? I haven't. I think it will be quite an experience for us both, don't you?'

He bounced up and down gently, then stood up and dragged off the maroon chenille cover, exposing half an acre of starched white linen.

The nervous tension she had felt all evening exploded into real fear.

'Look,' she ran her tongue round her dry lips, 'I'd much rather sleep at the farmhouse. Surely they can find room for me—anywhere will do. I'm not fussy.'

Raoul shook his head in apparent bewilderment. 'And yet, a while back, I had the distinct impression that you were not happy about spending a night in a barn. And anyway, I am sorry, I quite forgot to tell you. All five of the farmer's children have—what is it?—mumps.'

Feeling slightly sick, Jenni backed up against the wall, glad of its support, for her legs had suddenly become unsteady.

Raoul shot her a glance, then gave her a grin of pure devilment.

'Do not distress yourself, *ma petite*. Look,' He gestured towards the bedhead, where there was an uninviting, sausage-like bolster. 'This can lie between us, like the naked sword of chastity in former days, so——'

'No,' Jenni said loudly. 'I—I can't——'

She broke off and turned, blindly moving towards the door, but before she could escape Raoul was across the room and leaning against it, his arms folded. That quick movement, light as a hunting panther, jolted her into horrifying awareness of her situation. In the other room, fool that she was, jigsaws and a wood stove had made everything seem, if not secure, at least manageable. Here, though, with Raoul barring her way, there could be no escape until—until what? Her fingers played nervously among the folds of her dress.

'Let me past, please.' Her voice was high and strained, even to her own ears.

By way of reply, he lazily lifted one hand to trail his fingers down the side of her neck and on to the smooth swell of her breast. Jenni stood frozen for an instant, not breathing, then said again, in a gasp, 'Please—let me out.'

Raoul put one finger under her chin, turning her face up to his, then gently brushed away a tear which quivered on her lashes.

'Tch! What a child you are—all eyes and legs, like a young fawn in our park.' He gave her a faintly rueful smile. 'Do not be afraid of me, *ma petite*. I have never yet taken a woman by force. You shall have the bed all to yourself.'

He moved aside and opened the door. '*Voilà*. You will find the bathroom on the far side of the kitchen.'

In the bathroom, Jenni stared into the small mirror, gripping the washbasin hard to stem the quivering of her body. From the glass, though, her eyes mocked her, telling her the shameful truth: that when Raoul had touched her in that almost casual caress, despite her cold words, her whole being had shuddered with an intense, shameful desire for him.

Oh, damn! It just wasn't fair that, without the least effort and quite uncaring, he should have this almost shocking effect on her. She banged her hands down against the porcelain, then ran cold water into the basin, almost angrily, and again and again splashed it in handfuls on to her face and neck.

In the living-room, Raoul was standing near the stove, taking off his shirt. The powerful muscles in his shoulders were tensed as he turned to her, while his skin, gilded in the light from the flames, looked like polished satin. Jenni froze in the doorway, filled with such a longing for him that her legs almost began to move towards him of their own volition.

His eyes were on her and she saw again that consciousness flicker in them for an instant, but he merely raised one eyebrow slightly at the voluminous folds of white nightdress, remarking, 'Well, I suppose that Madame, with five children already, feels that anything more—provoking in the way of nightwear might perhaps be injudicious.'

He grinned at her, then draped a couple of blankets over the sofa and patted its unyielding contours.

'Mmm, horsehair,' he remarked conversationally. 'Well, it could be worse, I suppose—no doubt the floor would be even harder.'

An idea struck her. 'Those jigsaws! Surely there must be beds for the children who stay here.'

He gestured towards a large cupboard under the stairs. 'A cot, and a small child's bed—but, alas, it would not, I am sure, last the night even under your weight.'

'Well——' she hesitated '—I can sleep on the sofa. I'm smaller than you, and besides I sleep like a log anywhere.'

He grinned again. 'Very chivalrous, I am sure, and I am deeply touched. But no, off you go, please.'

In the great bed, her feet were cold as ice after the quarry-tiled floor of the bathroom. She drew her knees up to her chest, hugging herself, then stiffened as a dark bulk filled the doorway.

'Madame assured me that she aired the bed yesterday, but——'

He lifted a corner of the blanket and, as she lay motionless, slid an old-fashioned stone hot-water bottle down beside her.

'Not the most congenial of companions, I fear, but it will keep you warm.'

He pulled the covers up again and laid his hand lightly on her forehead. *'Bonne nuit, Jenni. Dors bien.'*

And he was gone before she could murmur her thanks.

The bottle was marvellously hot. She cuddled its hardness to her, then pushed it down to her feet. The bed grew warm as she relaxed and closed her eyes . . .

Two hours later, she still lay sleepless, watching the moonlight filter in through the shutters. She had a terrible, raging thirst, which could only be from the highly seasoned chicken dish they had eaten earlier that evening. Angrily, she thumped the pillow and flung herself over on to her other side. It did no good, though. Visions of glasses misted with icy-cold water still floated before her closed lids, and at length she sat up with a despairing groan. It was no use. She had to have a drink, even though Raoul literally lay between her and the kitchen, and he, she was quite certain, would sleep like a cat . . .

One of the stairs creaked horribly and she froze for long moments, but there was no movement from the direction of the sofa, and she was almost sure she could hear his regular breathing. She tiptoed silently across the room and through into the tiny kitchen, where she gulped down a glass of cold water, almost whimpering with relief, then refilled it to take back with her.

She had safely negotiated half the room when Raoul's voice came softly from the darkness, 'Have you come to make sure I am quite comfortable?' and the glass almost leaped from her hand.

'No, I—I was thirsty,' she faltered, then added accusingly, 'I thought you were asleep.'

'Asleep? *Mon Dieu*, just look at me!'

She gingerly went a few paces nearer the sofa until she could just make out its faint outline, and a large shape, half covered by a blanket, one long trousered leg dangling over the end, one stretched to the floor.

Jenni suppressed a nervous giggle, but then bit her lip, conscience-stricken.

'Look, Raoul,' she had begun to speak almost before she realised it, 'you can't possibly stay like this all night.' Without allowing herself to think, she hurried on, 'If you like, you can share the bed. As you said, we can put the bolster down the middle, and . . .' Her voice trailed away uncertainly.

He did not reply for a few moments, and she thought, oh, no, he's got the wrong idea. I should never have——

Raoul untangled himself from the embrace of the sofa and stood up slowly. In the dying flicker of the stove, seeing his dark hair ruffled, his gleaming skin, Jenni cursed all kind thoughts and wished even more that she had never left the relative security of that bed. But it was far too late now.

He straightened up with a groan, one hand to his neck, the other across his back. Then he caught sight of her standing as though turned to stone on the far side of the sofa, and laughed softly.

'Please—put your anxious mind at rest. After two hours on that medieval instrument of torture, I do not believe I am capable of ravishing you, even if I wished to. And besides, that appalling nightdress armours you more securely than a cast of chain mail.'

In the bedroom, she watched, once more stifling a ridiculous impulse to laugh, as Raoul arranged the bolster with mathematical precision down the exact centre of the bed, and lay down in his half. Only then did she self-consciously hitch up the white folds of flannelette and scramble up the other side, to slide down into the bed.

'Goodnight, Jenni.'

''Night.'

She ostentatiously turned on her side away from him and buried her nose in the pillow, but still sleep would not come. Her every nerve-end was tinglingly aware of Raoul's presence, and only when she heard his easy breathing did she allow her rigid body to relax its guard. Then, gradually, she too drifted off to sleep . . .

CHAPTER SEVEN

A NARROW streak of pale light roused her. Still half-asleep, Jenni rolled over lazily against the bolster, then jerked into full wakefulness and lay, her heart pounding unevenly under her ribs. But there was no answering movement. Raoul was still asleep.

Very gingerly, she raised herself on one elbow and peeped over the bolster. He was lying on his side, his dark head resting against his outflung arm, the crescent of unshaven stubble giving to his unguarded face an unexpected, almost endearing hint of defencelessness, and she stared at him for a long time, while strange, painful sensations played around her heart-strings.

But then, equally unexpectedly, she experienced a driving need to get away from him, to escape from this room, which had all at once become overpoweringly claustrophobic.

Her breath catching fearfully in her mouth, she eased herself out of bed, snatched up her clothes and noiselessly opened the door. Once dressed, she peered at the fluorescent hands of her watch, then groaned inwardly. Four-thirty. What in the world could she do, apart from sitting staring into the grey ruin of the previous evening's fire for perhaps a couple of hours?

Outside, though, the light was getting stronger every instant, and she had never been out of doors at dawn on a summer's morning . . . But when she tried the door, it was locked, and the key had been removed—no doubt, quite deliberately. She was to remain a prisoner until Raoul chose to wake. She bit her lip in vexation, then thought, the window, perhaps I can climb

92

out. She inched open the wooden shutters, then, holding her breath at every faint creak, hauled herself on to the sill and dropped lightly down into the damp grass.

Still on hands and knees, she dabbled her palms in the dew-whitened grass and rubbed them, silken-soft, over her face and bare arms, then stood up, the lush grass dragging gently against her legs and the hem of her dress.

A trodden path led through a gap in a nearby hedge, into another meadow dotted with scrubby hawthorn bushes, which were smothered with creamy-white blossom. She broke off a spray, sniffing its rich vanilla scent, and tucked it in her hair. Over in the far corner of the field, three biscuit-coloured cows were standing motionless among the moon daisies and butter-cups, as though on a child's two-dimensional nursery frieze.

It was a magical morning. The rim of the rising sun was already gilding the trees and grass, and an invisible bird sang from the depths of a tree. A line from her favourite school hymn came unbidden to her mind: 'Morning has broken, like the first morning . . .' If only she could hug this one moment to her, make it last for ever, she thought, and was taken unawares by the tight ache in her throat.

There was a rickety wooden bridge over a stream, and she perched on it, swinging her legs and idly following the erratic course of a shoal of speckled minnows.

All at once she glanced up and saw, with an intense, bewildering flash of joy, Raoul coming towards her across the meadow, with long, purposeful strides. She leaned back against the trunk of an overhanging willow, watching him as, second by second, he grew larger, and as he came closer a terrible sick hunger like a pain gripped her whole body.

At the same instant, a lightning flash of appalled realisation jagged through her brain. Oh no, she prayed, please, no, don't let me! But it was too late. The one thing which, consciously

or otherwise, she had struggled against ever since she had first
seen him, had happened. Now, she had to clench her fists into
her lap, until her nails bit deep, against the urge to run to him,
hurl herself bodily into his arms and cry, I love you, Raoul!

As he came up to her, half-unconsciously she lifted one hand
towards him, then hastily translated the movement to brush
back the damp fringe from her forehead, at the same time
smoothing away the inane smile while seemed to be
insidiously bursting out all over her face.

'Er—hello.'

Raoul formally inclined his head. 'Good morning, Jenni.'

His voice was grave, but she thought she detected a faint,
fleeting undertone of irony.

'H—how did you know where to find me?'

Raoul pointed to the dark, tell-tale trail of footprints through
the damp meadow grass, then said sternly, 'Your feet are wet.'

Jenni lowered her head and studied her slim, tanned feet,
shimmering with moisture and golden pollen dust, with
critical intensity, as though seeing them for the very first time.

'Why, yes—they are.'

'It's fortunate that I have your shoes.' And he held out the
white sandals to her.

'Oh, it really doesn't——' she began, but he put up a hand to
silence her.

'Please—I remember only too clearly that thistle last night.'

Before she could move, he shook out his folded handkerchief
and knelt in front of her. He took one foot, grasping it firmly
as she flinched back, then methodically wiped it dry, his dark
head bent over it. As she looked down at him, a surge of raw
emotion swept through her. Oh, my love, she thought, and
had to fight against the almost irresistible need to jump down
from the bridge and clutch him to her.

Sensing perhaps the tremor that ran through her whole

body, he looked up at her and she steeled herself for what he might say. But he merely smiled and asked indulgently, 'And what is going through your head now, *ma petite?*'

That I love you, that I can't live without you! The words cried out in her head, yet somehow, miraculously, she found herself sliding her foot into the sandal and saying, in what sounded very like her normal tone, 'Oh, I was just thinking that I feel like Cinderella.'

Raoul buckled the thin strap. 'You know, of course, the interesting symbolism that lies behind that charming fairy story?' He shot her a quick glance, then smiled. 'No—I think you do not. One day, perhaps, I will tell you.'

He started on the other foot. 'So—if you are Cinderella, I must be Prince Charming. Although,' his voice was dry, 'I should imagine that your opinion of me extends more in the direction of the—what was it?—the lizard footman.'

'Oh, no,' Jenni replied demurely, shooting him a quick look under the sweep of her lashes, 'more like the coachman, I think. What was he? Oh, yes, a rat!'

'Why, you little——' Raoul laughed out loud, then dropped her foot and leaped up.

Jenni had time for just one squeal of terror before she over-balanced and toppled backwards. It was not a great fall, but she landed helplessly on her back, with a gasp of shock, in two feet of cold, muddy water.

She was vaguely aware of Raoul's horrified face, then he had vaulted over the plank which propped up one end of the bridge and was standing on the bank, holding out both hands. he clasped hers in a strong grip, and with a horrible slurping sound she rose unsteadily to her feet and stood on the bank beside him, her heels sinking gently into the mud.

'Are you hurt?'

There was real anxiety in Raoul's voice, and Jenni did a

lightning mental inspection of the various parts of her
anatomy.

'No, I'm all right.'

He leaned forward and delicately plucked a strand of
duckweed from her arm.

'I'm sorry, Jenni. It was my fault.'

'Well, maybe it serves me right for calling you a rat.'

Their eyes met and then, feeling all at once the ridicu-
lousness of her situation, she grinned at him. Raoul's lips
twitched, then a moment later they had both dissolved into
helpless laughter, Jenni forced to clutch his arm to steady
herself. She was still laughing when she felt him snatch her
up into his arms.

'No!' She kicked wildly. 'You'll be soaked too.'

He looked down at her, the laugher still dancing in his
eyes. 'What? And me, a mere mortal, miss the only
opportunity in my life to carry Aphrodite after she has risen
from the waves?'

Unable quite to respond to the new, teasing tone in his
voice, she gave him a shy, uncertain smile. But then the
amusement faded abruptly from his eyes and they darkened
with an expression that she had never seen in them before
and which she found deeply disturbing. She looked quickly
away again, all too conscious now of his nearness, so near
that she could see the damp tide creeping across his white
shirt-front as he effortlessly retraced their path to the *gîte*.

He shouldered open the door, then carried her through
into the kitchen and set her down, little rivulets of water
dripping gently from the hem of her dress to patter on to
the tiled floor. She glanced down, then coloured involuntarily, as she realised for the first time that the wet folds of
cotton were clinging revealingly to every line and contour
of her body.

'Go and have a hot shower. Let me have your clothes and I will wash them out and hang them in the sun.'

In the minute bathroom, Jenni peeled off the sopping wet dress and handed it out through the barely opened door.

'And the rest, please.'

Raoul still held out his hand, so, after a fractional hesitation, she thrust out the little sodden heap of cream lace and cotton.

After her shower, she wrapped herself in the largest bath towel she could find, although an alarming amount of tanned flesh still seemed to be all too visible. When she ventured out, though, Raoul was nowhere to be seen and the front door was wide open. She flew through the living-room, up the stairs, and had just finished draping herself in the voluminous though scratchy folds of the chenille counterpane when Raoul, stripped to the waist, appeared in the doorway holding in his hand two mugs.

'Your clothes will dry in the sun, but it will take some time.'

'Oh.'

Jenni sat up carefully as he came across the room and sat down on the edge of the bed.

'You should have a hot drink.'

He held out a steaming mug and, clutching the bedspread to her, she slid out one hand and took the coffee.

'Thank you.'

They drank in silence—a seemingly relaxed, even companionable silence on Raoul's part. Jenni, though, her perceptions heightened sharply since she had acknowledged to herself the depths of her feelings for him, sensed, so faint as to be almost imperceptible, an eddy of tension about the room. She drained her mug quickly, hardly aware of the burning liquid, and he took it from her. He set both mugs

on the floor, then, as he sat back, they regarded each other
for long moments in silence. At last he spoke.

'You have petals caught in your hair. Keep still.'

He leaned towards her and carefully picked out the tiny
shreds of white. He dropped them into his palm, then blew
softly so that they drifted down on to the floor, in a tiny
snowstorm. As though hypnotised, Jenni watched them
slowly fall, then dragged her eyes away to meet Raoul's
again.

'That mass of hair,' he began slowly, as though musing to
himself, 'it gives a Pre-Raphaelite look.'

He put his hand under her chin and gently tilted her face
up, then gave her an odd smile.

'Do you know what that means?'

His touch, though feather-light, and the expression in his
eyes, were deeply disturbing again, and she could only
shake her head slowly.

'Your face has intrigued me since the first time I saw you.
You are like Philippe, of course, although I did not at first
realise that. You have the same look,' he frowned slightly,
'of a tamed wild creature, which somewhere retains a hint
of wildness. But you also resemble one of the Rossetti
paintings which we have in the château.'

Jenni stared at him, feeling a hard, agonising lump swell
in her throat. She swallowed it down and said in a low
voice, 'I—I didn't realise that you knew him so well.'

He shrugged. 'As to that, I hardly did. He was many
years older.'

'What was he like?'

He did not reply at once, then, as if in response to the
half-conscious yearning in her voice, said slowly, 'As I told
you—wild.' He smiled reminiscently. 'I remember that his
method of teaching me to ride was to set me astride his

hunter, put the reins into my hands and slap the horse's rump. But I adored him—everyone did—because under the wildness, the *joie de vivre*, there was a——' he hesitated, as though feeling for the correct word '—a goodness, even a nobility of character. And besides,' he pulled a wry face, 'when I fell off the horse and broke my arm, it was he who gave me my first puppy.'

Tight-lipped, Jenni stared past him, unable to respond to his smile. Shadows of the past peopled every corner of the room. A laughing young man placed a child on a horse and raised his hand to set them galloping. She remembered the crumpled photograph, the radiant, smiling girl, hardly older than she herself. Without warning, there were scalding tears in her eyes. She bit her lip, then, as her hands flew to her face, the tears brimmed over, pouring down her cheeks. Raoul, with an incoherent exclamation, pulled her to him. She went awkwardly into his arms and he enfolded her, as terrible, racking sobs began to shake her whole body. He cradled her against him, stroking her hair and rocking her gently, until at last the sobs died away and she lay still, apart from the occasional quivering sigh.

Raoul eased her from him and tilted her face towards him.

'And have you cried all your sorrow out now, *ma petite?*'

Jenni managed a watery smile in response to his serious expression. 'Y—yes. I'm sorry. I haven't cried like that since I was a little girl.'

'You can be proud of him, you know, but——' He was silent for so long that she looked at him enquiringly. 'You must not try to call back the past. There is a wise saying: let the dead bury the dead. You are young and alive. Well, let the past go from you, *non?*'

Jenni drew a long, shuddering breath. Full circle. She

had followed a painful, tortuous route, but now, in this warm, shadowed room, she felt as though she had finally come full circle. The search was ended: she could begin to live, totally free for the first time. And meanwhile Raoul was watching her, with that grave smile which she so loved crinkling the corners of his eyes.

'Thank you.'

He gave a self-deprecating half-shrug. 'For what?'

'Oh, I don't know.' She didn't seem able to express herself in words. 'Just thank you.'

She smiled at him and stretched out her hand in a spontaneous gesture. He took it between both of his and held it for a moment, his eyes on her face. Then, very slowly, he lowered his head and began sliding his warm lips across her moist palm and along the length of each finger, until he reached her thumb. He raised his head slightly and they stared into each other's eyes for what seemed to Jenni an endless, heart-stopping time, then with infinite gentleness he drew her towards him. Afterwards, she realised that he had been giving her every opportunity to resist him if she had wished, but instead she smiled tremulously at him and made no attempt to break free.

Raoul drew in his breath harshly and one hand tightened over hers as he brought the other up to cup her head. His kiss was slow and gentle at first, though it rapidly deepened in intensity as she, lost to all conscious thought, to everything except the singing joy of being in his arms, opened her lips to his.

When he lifted her away from him a little, she gave a tiny murmur of protest, but it was only to ease down the folds of chenille from her shoulders.

'*Mon Dieu*! What have you done?'

Following his shocked eyes, she saw that he was staring at

the huge bruise, still faintly purple, which disfigured one shoulder.

'Oh, they threw me against the wall when they snatched my bag. It's almost gone now, and it doesn't hurt, honestly.'

She gave him a reassuring smile as he gazed at her with a strange expression in his eyes.

His lips tightened and he said sombrely, 'How I have misjudged you, *ma pauvre petite.*'

She closed her eyes as his mouth brushed delicately across the centre of the bruise, then kept them closed as she felt his hands pulling the counterpane away from her and laying her down on the bed. When she opened them again, her naked body, slim and tanned against the whiteness of the sheet, was curved into the bed. She gave a faint gasp and brought up one arm across her breasts in an instinctive, protective gesture, then looked up and saw that Raoul was watching her, a small, gentle smile of complete understanding on his face.

'Do not be afraid, Jenni,' he said softly, and raising his hand he caressed her face, then her shoulder and down across her stomach to her thigh, in a movement at once infinitely tender yet totally, intimately possessive, which left her quivering softly as new, bewildering sensations erupted all over her body.

As Raoul undressed she turned away, but then, as he lay beside her, he turned her head back towards him, though she would not meet his eyes.

'Jenni.'

'Y—yes.' It was hardly more than a whisper.

'You have a beautiful body. You must learn not to be ashamed of it or to fear its power.'

His fingers trailed a tingling line down her shoulder and

on to the arm which still enfolded her breasts, prickling the
fine down of golden hairs on her skin, so that she felt them
stand on end under his touch. Gently but irresistibly, that
protective arm was drawn away and his lips were caressing
her breasts until, with a throaty gasp of pleasure, she felt
them stir into life beneath the insistent touch of his
tongue.

His hands moved on, lingering, endlessly caressing,
returning, circling ever nearer to the secret, shimmering
centre of her being. Flames were smouldering all through
her body, bursting into forest fires under his touch, so that
it seemed to scorch her flesh. With an incoherent murmur,
hardly aware of what she was doing, she put her arms
around him, her hands splayed against the heated skin of
his back, and drew him closer, the whole length of her soft
body straining against the whiplash tautness of his in mute
appeal.

At this innocent betrayal of herself to him, Raoul gave a
choked groan and turned his face to her shoulder, his
unshaven chin rough against the tender skin, while the faint
aroma of soap and male body made her senses reel.

Although he moved with careful compassion, there was
pain at first, a sharp, swift thrust of pain. She buried her
face against his chest to stifle the little cry that would have
escaped her, but he sensed the movement and kissed the top
of her head with low, murmured endearments. But then the
pain was past and her clenched muscles relaxed to him. A
wholly new, overwhelming rapture was engulfing her,
every fibre of her being melting into the overpowering
need to be one with him, until she cried out, against his
shoulder, and felt the intense shudder which ran through
his body.

Long afterwards, she lay drowsily cradled in his arms,

and thought, over and over again, please, oh please, let him love me too.

CHAPTER EIGHT

THE ROLLING woodlands, that pretty cottage . . . nothing had changed, and when Jenni stared at her ghost reflection in the car window she too, incredibly, looked exactly the same.

She shot Raoul a covert glance, but he seemed preoccupied, as he had been ever since they had left the *gîte*. He had roused her from a dreamless slumber with her dress, now dried, had announced briefly that the car was mobile, after all, and now, just one short hour later, they were approaching Les Forêts. All his attention appeared to be on the road, so she could study him in safety, the untidy black hair, the dark stubble, now long past a five o'clock shadow, and heart-wrenchingly attractive . . . Her colour deepened, as her breathing quickened uncomfortably . . .

His expression, though, had assumed a distant, even forbidding quality, and all at once the long silence which had hung between them became oppressive and she turned away. That remote, enchanted barn was somewhere in another time warp, and now—to what was she returning? No job and—she bit her lip—Raoul seemed able effortlessly to compartmentalise his life; was the episode between them earlier that morning to be filed away in yet another convenient compartment? Yes—the stab of real pain caught her unawares—for Raoul was surely not the sort of man to let a transitory romantic interlude elbow its way into real life. So in that case——

'You look sad, *ma petite*.' Raoul took his eyes from the road long enough to give her a swift, searching look. He pulled a mock derisory face. 'Even regretful. Please—you will severely dent my self-esteem. Or perhaps it is that you are mourning the innocence you lost in that feather bed?'

'Oh, no—er, at least,' she crimsoned, 'if—if you must know, I was wondering exactly how soon we shall start fighting again.'

'Well, that depends.' His tone was ironically reflective.

'On what?'

'Oh, merely on whether from now onwards you accede to my views easily—or after a struggle.'

'But I shall give in, you mean?'

He raised his shoulder in the slightest of shrugs. 'But of course.'

She looked away from him, a small knot of unhappiness gathering in her stomach. No, nothing had changed. She reached for her bag.

'I'd rather you dropped me near the reception area, please. I'll walk through to my apartment from there.'

'Why?'

Faint anger began to stir in her.

'Because I prefer to,' she said shortly. Surely even he should understand that, having both been absent all that night, she would now rather reappear alone, although she was resigned to the knowing looks? Besides, her mind ached for a little solitude, for the chance to sort out her tumbled emotions into some sort of order.

But Raoul, as though he had not heard her, drove round to the back of the château and parked in the courtyard. Jenni's lips tightened. So he was going to be difficult, was he? Well, she would just walk all the way from here. As she went to open the door, though, his hand arrested hers, quite gently, but firmly. She sat quite still.

'Let me go, please. I want to get back to my apartment.'

In spite of her determination to betray no emotion, her voice shook at the touch of his hand on hers. She desperately wanted him to pull her into his arms, to murmur once more those endearments which she was beginning almost to believe she had imagined. But instead——

'Well, now,' Raoul's voice was reflective, 'that might be a little—inconvenient, Jenni. You see, Marie-Christine might not be too happy to find you on her territory.' And when she stared at him, her eyes darkening with horrified suspicion, he went on, 'I see you understand the situation perfectly. And, after all, the poor girl had to have somewhere to lay her head.'

'So, before we even left yesterday, you had given her my apartment.' It was more a flat statement of fact than a question.

He spread his hands in a gesture of wholehearted apology, but she was not fooled for an instant. Her job yesterday, her flat today.

'And precisely what plans do you have in mind for me? You understand, I ask merely for information.' The anger and pain that he should want to treat her like this mingled to put a honed edge to her voice.

'You will see.'

Raoul got out, then opened her door. One hand under her elbow, he opened a door, then guided her through a maze of unused rooms which had once obviously been the château kitchens and store-rooms. In a passage, they came face to face with an elderly, grey-haired woman in a navy dress.

'*Bonjour, Madame Cherbay.*' To Jenni, still in French, he said, 'Madame is our invaluable housekeeper.'

He smiled at the woman. 'Would you take Mademoiselle Eugénie up to her suite?'

His grip tightened like steel as Jenni stiffened. Then, as she stared at him, his eyes flashed a silent warning and she closed her mouth tightly. However great her desire might be to leap at him and rend him bodily limb from limb, she certainly was not going to demean herself before an interested spectator.

'That is better, *ma chère*. Remember—no resistance, I beg you.' His voice was for her ears alone, then he said more loudly, 'I have some phone calls to make. Please bring *Mademoiselle* to my office when she is ready.' And he turned on his heel and strode off through the swing doors, leaving Jenni glowering silently after him.

'If you will come with me, Mademoiselle Eugénie.'

The well-schooled face showed no curiosity, not even a polite interest in her crumpled, dishevelled appearance. Jenni hitched up her shoulder-bag and followed the housekeeper up a long flight of stairs, narrower than those in the front hall, but still impressive, and along the length of a wide passage, lined by tables adorned with chill-eyed marble busts and lit from above by skylights. They passed one door which stood ajar, and she had a glimpse of white-shrouded furniture in a gloomy half-light.

Madame Cherbay opened a door at the end of the passage and ushered her in. The room was very large, yet the immediate sensation it produced on Jenni was oppressive. It was crowded with furniture—heavily carved sideboards, huge high-backed wooden chairs and dark side tables; all old yet ugly, with no antique charm. From this room a door led into a bedroom, again filled with furniture chosen as though for the reassurance of ostentatious wealth rather than comfort, Jenni thought, including a wide bed under an overhanging carved lintel of a bedhead.

Through an open door, she could see a huge bathroom

with polished mahogany fittings, while beyond the
bedroom was a small, dark kitchen, its modern stove and
electric kettle somehow incongruous. Jenni returned slowly
to the sombre bedroom and stood looking around her as her
own reflection stared back from the mirror in the mahogany
dressing-table, wide-eyed, apprehensive.

Something of her feelings must have communicated
themselves to the other woman, for she said, 'I hope you
will be comfortable, *mademoiselle*. I have done my best.'
And indeed Jenni, looking round her, could see a little posy
of pink rosebuds on the bedside-table, a shaggy sheepskin
rug beside the bed, and through in the bathroom a pile of
fluffy yellow towels. 'But Monsieur Raoul was insistent
that you were put in here.'

She stopped then, as though afraid she had said too much,
and Jenni said quickly, 'Thank you, I shall be very
comfortable, I'm sure.'

A relieved smile flickered across the woman's face. 'And
if I may just say so, *mademoiselle,*' the words came in rather
a rush, 'we are all so very happy to have Monsieur
Philippe's daughter with us.' She gave Jenni a warm smile.
'And now, if you are ready, I am to take you down to
Monsieur Raoul.'

Jenni darted her a quick look, then sat down very deliberately on the edge of the bed and sniffed at the bowl of roses.
'Mmm, they smell lovely—thank you so much.'

She smiled, adding casually, 'I'm not quite ready to come
down yet, so you go on without me.'

Madame Cherbay hovered uncertainly near the door, and
opened her mouth as though to protest, but then, as Jenni
flashed her what she hoped was a supremely confident
smile, she nodded with the barest gleam of an answering,
admiring smile in her eyes, then retreated, closing the door

softly.

Jenni let out her breath in a long sigh of relief. One small, infinitesimal battle won. She had not, after all, obediently trotted down at Raoul's bidding, ready to touch her forelock in humble submission.

She leaned back against the unyielding bedhead and surveyed the room. Now that she was quite alone, it seemed even larger, yet even more oppressive, its silence weighing on her spirits. Once again, she felt herself being snared, unable to break free from a limed trap. A line from an old music-hall song tinkled in her mind; 'Only a bird in a gilded cage'. She stood up abruptly, picked up her bag and went through to the bathroom.

She ran some warm water into the gargantuan washbasin and splashed her face and hands, then combed her hair and surveyed herself critically. There was nothing to be done about her grubby dress, but under her tan she had a pallor which some people might construe as nervousness, so she rubbed on some blusher, then added a brighter pink lipgloss than usual.

She was replacing the lipstick top when she stopped suddenly, wide-eyed with shock. It was surely her own toothbrush and paste that stood in the china mug, and yes—her face flannel and sponge. The cabinet was slightly open and, when she looked inside, there were her toilet preparations lined on the shelves.

She flew back into the bedroom and snatched open the heavy wardrobe door. Inside, in an orderly row at one end of the cavernous cupboard, on padded hangers which smelt of southernwood and lavender, were her clothes, her sweaters neatly folded on shelves lined with white tissue.

Jenni stared at them in disbelief. How could he? How dared he? Then she gave a faint, bitter smile. What a stupid question. Very easily, of course . . .

Eventually, after a search of the ground floor, she found
him in an attractive, modern pine kitchen. In the short time
that she had been upstairs, he had shaved and was now
wearing charcoal-grey, casual, tight-fitting cords and a
silky, pale blue, roll-neck sweater, and Jenni wished
momentarily that she had taken time off from her anger to
change quickly. He was now back to his suavely immaculate
best, while the faintest aroma of muddy water seemed to
hang still about her dress.

The round pine table was set for two, a basket with a long
loaf cut into hunks and an opened bottle of red wine and
two glasses standing at one end. Raoul was grilling two
huge steaks and did not turn as she went in.

'Good. I was afraid that I would have to come and look
for you. I hope that you do not object to eating *en famille*.'

'H—how dare you?' Jenni was barely able to articulate the
words.

He glanced round, one quizzical eyebrow raised. 'Oh, I
am sorry. I thought a steak would be to your liking, but if
you would prefer——'

His wilful misunderstanding only enraged her more and
she cut in, 'You know very well what I mean. My clothes—
all my belongings, my personal possessions. And don't tell
me you had nothing to do with it. In this place, no one
would have dared lay a finger on them without your express
permission.'

He gave her a cool look. 'I have told you,' he began, with
deliberate patience, as though reasoning with a recalcitrant
child, 'Marie-Christine has returned. I am sure, if you allow
yourself to think calmly about it, you would not wish your
possessions to remain in her apartment.'

Jenni shook her head in angry frustration. Short of a

physical assault, which she was bound to lose anyway, there was simply no way to get through to this man.

'But you didn't ask me—you just did it.'

Raoul flipped the steaks over deftly. 'I presume, like most *Anglais*, you wish your steaks to be grilled into boot leather?'

'And anyway, *if* I have to move out——' she realised that she was rapidly giving ground, but endeavouring to stand up to Raoul, she thought despairingly, was rather like attempting to stem the tide, and King Canute had discovered just what a futile exercise that was '—I won't live in those rooms. I—I don't like them.'

'That is unfortunate,' he remarked gravely, although she was almost positive that there was a malicious glint at the back of those steely eyes. 'I thought it only fitting that you should have your grandmother's apartment. As a second Eugénie Aimée, you surely have some slight feeling for it. Oh, yes,' he went on as she stared at him, 'did Madame Cherbay not tell you? When your grandmother became an invalid, that was her suite of rooms.' He calmly set a bowl of tossed salad on the table.

Jenni licked her drip lips. 'Did—did she die there?'

'But of course. That was her bed.' His eyes narrowing, he went on, 'Surely such a forthright young woman as you does not believe in ghosts.'

'I am not sleeping in that room,' Jenni said loudly, and banged her hand down smartly on the table in emphasis. 'I—I hate it, all that horrible furniture and that bed. It's—it's got a death's head carved on it.'

Raoul sighed dramatically. 'Tch! What ingratitude. To refuse the opportunity to sleep under a priceless seventeenth-century Spanish headboard.'

'I don't care,' she repeated stubbornly at his back as he served up the steaks. 'I tell you, I'm not sleeping there.'

He put the plates on the table and gestured her to sit, then glanced at his watch. 'Eat, please. Our lawyer, François David, will be here in an hour.'

The meal was excellent and Jenni should have been ravenous, but she could only toy with it, chewing a little with difficulty and distributing the rest around her plate, in silence, and avoiding Raoul's eyes as her busy mind endeavoured to work out all eventualities. But it was no use. In every train of thought she came up hard against the brick wall of Raoul and what he intended for her . . .

She refused his offer of strawberries and rich yellow cream, and sat on in silence as he ate with every appearance of appetite, until at last he wiped his lips with his napkin and pushed back his chair.

'And now, you do not like the furnishings in your suite. *Bien,* you are at liberty to make what changes you wish, to your own taste. I will show you my apartment and you will see that these rooms can be made very comfortable.'

Jenni followed him from the kitchen across the passage into a sitting-room, a pleasant, sun-filled room. The pale wood furniture was modern, the sofa and club chairs cream leather. The dog she had seen in the *salon* the previous day was curled up on the rug in a mound of silky beige and brown fur, and when they went in he got up and stretched himself lazily, then went over to Jenni and nuzzled at her hand. She stooped down and caressed the soft head and back, and he put a paw up to her shoulder, melting brown eyes gazing at her through a honey-coloured fringe. She looked past him to Raoul.

'He's absolutely beautiful. What's his name?'

'Igor. He is a borzoi, a Russian imperial hunting dog. He's quite an old dog now, getting very stiff in the joints.'

He looked down at the dog, gently snapping his fingers,

and the animal immediately left Jenni and went to him, pushing against his legs affectionately.

'He has to be banished from the kitchen when I am cooking. He may come from emperor stock, but I am afraid he is just a thieving mongrel where steak is concerned.' He wagged his finger at Igor in mock severity then rumpled the dog's head, so that Jenni sensed an almost tangible bond of love between man and dog.

'And now,' resumed Raoul, 'my office.'

The book-lined room was untidy, the huge desk littered with papers, ledgers and hastily opened mail, together with a telephone and answering machine. But, despite the apparent disorder, Jenni guessed that this was the real heart of the estate.

Igor padded off down the corridor and, pushing his head against the far door, nosed it open.

'I see Igor is intent on giving you a full guided tour of my bachelor establishment,' Raoul commented drily. 'He obviously wishes you to inspect my bedroom.'

Jenni hesitated in the doorway, but his hand gave her a gentle push. This room showed a sternly masculine disregard for softness, though it still managed to exude an air of comfort. The chests of drawers and wardrobe, though clearly antique, were smaller and lighter than those in the apartment upstairs. The large bed was modern, and covered by a bedspread in heavy embossed terracotta cotton, a shade which picked up the warm, earthy tints of the carpet and curtains.

On one wall was an almost life-sized portrait in oils, in a heavy gilded frame. Something about the painting drew Jenni towards it. She walked slowly over and studied it intently. The artist—a first-class one, she realised—had set his subjects with artful carelessness against a background of fields and—yes, surely it was Les Forêts behind them? The young man, with a shock of brown hair, in open-necked shirt and Norfolk jacket, leaned against the stile, his gun propped beside him, a casually affectionate hand laid across the knees of the dark-haired child who was perched at his side. At their feet was a borzoi hound.

'I remember the painter had terrible problems with Philippe.' Raoul spoke from across the room. 'He was always disappearing, gun in hand, after half an hour or so of every sitting. His mother used to be furious with him.'

Jenni felt one spasm of sadness for the bright young life, so soon to be cruelly snuffed out, but then thrust the feeling from her. 'And is—is that Igor?'

Raoul laughed. 'No, that was Boris, the puppy your father gave me as conscience payment when he broke my arm. But Igor is his son. You recognise the boy, of course?'

Jenni had done no more than glance at the child. Now, though, when she studied the portrait again, there was something—the half-smile, that lock of dark hair across the boy's brow.

'It's you, isn't it?' She turned to him.

'Yes, it is.' He pulled a wry face. 'A long time ago, I'm afraid. What is it your English poet called them—days of innocence?'

Jenni took a last, lingering look at the painting, then walked over to the high windows. She gazed out, her eyes travelling across the softly rolling fields and woodlands, then all at once became very aware of a shadow behind her in the glass, of Raoul's warm breath on her neck. They both stood motionless, as though locked into some bubble of timelessness, Jenni hardly breathing, until Igor, obviously sensing the invisible, spiralling tension around him, whined softly then pattered out of the room.

'Yes, you're right,' she began inconsequentially, forcing herself to speak in an effort to break that tightening thread. 'You've made your apartment very attractive.'

'Well,' his voice was a soft, intimate murmur in her ear, 'if you really find this place so *agréable,* you could always, of course, live here.'

Jenni spun round. 'Oh, no!' she blurted out. 'It's very generous of you, but I couldn't possibly allow you to move out for me.'

He spread his hands in a half-apologetic gesture, but there was light mockery in his eyes. 'Alas, *ma petite,* you misunderstand me. This has been my apartment since I came of age, and I have no intention whatever of moving out.'

She stared at him, appalled, her face flooding with angry, mortified colour. What a naïve fool he must think her! After the scene in the *gîte* that morning, he obviously had assumed, not only that she would have not the faintest hesitation in accepting his offer, but that she would leap at it. In fact, now she thought about it, the whole episode of her grandmother's suite had probably been no more than an elaborate charade. He had never had the least intention of installing her in that gloomy barracks upstairs, correctly calculating that its effect would be to send her scuttling down like a frightened rabbit to him.

'Oh, no,' she set her chin proudly, although she could not prevent her voice from quivering slightly, 'whatever this—this morning may have led you to believe, I have no intention of becoming your m-mistress.'

'And is the thought of becoming the mistress of Raoul Kerouac so utterly repugnant to you, Jenni?'

He raised one hand and very gently traced round the outline of her lips with his finger. She tensed, trying desperately to suppress the shiver which ran through her at his sensuous touch, so that she hardly heard him as he went on, his voice perfectly serious, no hint of any secret amusement in his grey eyes now.

'But in any case, *ma chère*, you have jumped rather too quickly to the wrong conclusion. I was not asking you to enter into some little liaison which doubtless to your mind would appear no more than a sordid intrigue. I am asking you to become my wife.'

Jenni gaped at him wordlessly for a long moment, then turned away abruptly. She realised that she was trembling, and leaned her hands against the cool window to try to steady herself. Raoul made no further move to touch her; she saw him behind her, mirrored in the glass, arms folded. She stared into that impassive, reflected face, her own thoughts a swirling maelstrom.

Her eyes wandered across the undulating countryside, Les Forêts land as far as she could see, and for a moment she saw herself, *châtelaine* of Les Forêts . . . working side by side with Raoul, helping him build up the estate's prosperity, not just as his co-heir, his partner, reluctantly taken because of an enforced legal quirk, but—her pulses leaped—as his wife.

Many women, she knew, would seize on his offer joyfully, with no further demands—what was it the young waitress had said—'They're all mad for him'?—but for her, could this be enough? No. All her life she had craved love, a craving born of her mother's indifference and, later, her stepfather's rejection, and she knew, by some potent, almost primitive instinct, that to be truly fulfilled she must be the beloved centre of another's being.

But if she married Raoul, would she—could she be that centre? Was it remotely possible that he could feel anything approaching genuine love for her, when less than two days before he had looked at her with such naked hatred and contempt? And yet . . . her eyes grew dreamy . . . he had been so tender, so gentle with her . . . As for herself, she only knew that her whole self ached to be in his arms once again. Of course, there had been other women in his life; she had to be worldly-wise enough to accept that. But if she did marry him, somehow—she set her lips in a determined line—somehow, inexperienced girl though she was, she would make him forget all other women . . .

And after all, Raoul had no need to marry her. True, she had the half-share in the estate, but how much real control would she have over its management, if she ever had the temerity to pit herself against him? None at all, she ruefully acceded. Whatever nominal rights she might have, Raoul in the end would always overrule, outmanoeuvre her—and he, of course, was fully as aware of that as she. In that case, then, there was absolutely no need at all for him to marry her, and therefore—her heart lifted with an ecstatic, incredulous joy—therefore . . .

Slowly, she turned to face him, and raised her eyes to meet his intent gaze. 'Do you love me?'

With a smothered exclamation, Raoul snatched her to him. '*Ma petite,*' he murmured against her ear, 'what a foolish question!'

He held her back at arm's length from him and gave her a smile that made her heart somersault painfully under her ribs. 'Well? You are clearly such a little romantic.' His eyes were half laughing, half serious. 'Do I therefore have to go down on both knees?'

'No, Raoul, you don't have to do that.' Her voice was amazingly steady. 'I will marry you.'

CHAPTER NINE

JENNI added her neat signature to the document, then pushed it back across the desk to Monsieur David, smiling at him as she did so. He was a nice man, she thought—not at all the sort of dry stick she would have imagined the estate lawyer to be.

When he had arrived, he had shaken her warmly by the hand, saying, 'My dear child, I cannot tell you the pleasure it gives me to see Philippe's child at Les Forêts.'

He shuffled through the pile of documents, gathered them up and slid them into his leather briefcase as Jenni leaned back in her chair.

'And that's all I have to do, Monsieur David?' She shook her head in disbelief. The events of the past two hours—events which would change the entire shape and pattern of her life for ever—had left her bewildered, almost dazed. 'It just seems so—oh, I don't know,' she spread her hands, 'so ridiculously simple. Just half a dozen papers—is that really all?'

The two men exchanged a glance, almost, she thought with fleeting puzzlement, as though some hidden message flashed between them, but then the lawyer smiled at her. 'Yes, that is really all, *mademoiselle.*'

'Well, not quite all, François.' Raoul was behind her, his hand firmly on her shoulder. 'You see, Jenni has just done me the honour of agreeing to be my wife, and so perhaps you would be kind enough to begin to draw up the necessary documents.'

118

Just for a second, there was a shrewd, even speculative, look in the lawyer's professionally bland eyes as he looked at her over his spectacles, but then he said, 'And what could be more *convenable?* I congratulate you, Raoul, and you also, my dear.' He gave Jenni a wry half-smile. 'Les Forêts could do with a little real happiness, I think, and you, I am sure, will be the young woman to bring it.'

Yes, yes, I will, she thought fiercely, then, meeting the eyes of the young hairdresser in the mirror, she smiled self-consciously and looked down, smoothing the folds of her pale yellow crêpe dress. It was one of several which Raoul, immediately after their engagement, had insisted on buying her, having expressed a pungent opinion of her present wardrobe. He had taken her to the most exclusive dress shop in Vannes and personally supervised the purchases, leaning back, hands in pockets, on a small, spindly chair, for all the world like some lordly pasha, she had thought, a touch resentfully, as she was paraded around the velvety carpeted show-ring for his approbation. In the end, though, he had softened sufficiently to indulge her with two pairs of denim jeams, though jeans with a difference, she had realised as, wide-eyed, she stared first at the tiny price tag, then at the label sewn inside the waistband.

He had also allowed her, in the face of her pleas, to keep her van, contenting himself merely with getting René to give it a thorough overhaul and spray over the happy dolphins, and had also not insisted, after all, on her moving into her grandmother's gloomy apartment. Instead, Madame Cherbay had tentatively suggested that *Mademoiselle* might prefer the child's turret suite until their marriage. When Raoul showed it to her, Jenni fell in love with it on sight. It consisted only of two rooms, their circular walls panelled in

pale oak; a small sitting-room, and above, after they had
climbed a narrow, winding stone staircase, a bedroom with
white-painted child's furniture and a tiny bathroom.

Jenni had clasped her hands in unfeigned delight. 'Oh,
Raoul, it's absolutely perfect. Please may I live here?'

'Of course. Though you are not intending to take up
residence here for ever, I trust?'

Jenni had looked at him from under her lashes, then, at
his half-humorous, half-tender expression, had turned
away, her face warm, to study the view through the small
lancet window very intently. In a mere two weeks—for
Raoul had insisted impatiently that the wedding take place
without delay—she would be downstairs, living in his
apartment, sharing his bed . . .

The hairdresser held up a mirror and Jenni studied her
own flushed reflection, then nodded and smiled her delight.
'Thank you, it's lovely.'

The girl, young though she was, must be a wizard with
the scissors. All the shaggy remnants of perm had vanished,
in their place a smooth, chin-length bob; and the henna
conditioning rinse had given her brown hair, as the
shampooist had promised, a wonderful gloss, lit by reddish-
gold glints.

Jenni glimpsed herself again in the opulent gilt mirror
behind the front desk—gleaming hair, suntanned face and
arms, pink-tipped nails, expensive dress. What a magical
transformation had been performed in hardly more than
days! And yet, despite the superficial gloss, she was still,
underneath, uncomfortably aware of her youth, her
gaucheness.

As she rested her bag on the counter, her eye was caught
by the green fire of the square-cut emerald engagement ring
in its dark gold setting, and the thought came to her

suddenly, will it all vanish at midnight? If I pinch myself hard enough, could I still wake up and find it was all a dream? She smiled at the immaculate stranger in the mirror, then thought, of course you won't. Amazing, incredible as it must seem to everyone, including yourself, Raoul loves you, doesn't he? And that's all that matters.

'. . . and Véronique will of course come early tomorrow,' the proprietress of the chic, perfumed salon was speaking. 'She will arrange your hair and head-dress.'

'Yes, thank you.' Jenni smiled at her confidently, while privately she thought, with a tinge of irony, that this must be what being rich was all about; although perfectly capable of pinning up her own hair, she must not be allowed to perform this menial task.

'Of course, *mademoiselle*, you have disappointed us, you know.' *Madame* shook her elegantly coiffured head reprovingly. 'A quiet wedding in the village church, not the cathedral—tch, tch!'

'But we decided that we would prefer it that way,' Jenni protested. In fact, Raoul had suggested it, and she had been only too relieved to escape from what she had feared would be an overpoweringly elaborate ceremony.

'But my dear *mademoiselle*, surely you must appreciate that the entire *département* is wild with curiosity to see Raoul Kerouac's bride?' She gave Jenni an arch glance, which she found strangely repellent, then added, 'And particularly the women, of course . . .'

The street was hot after the air-conditioned luxury of the salon, and Jenni stood hesitantly outside, trying to decide what to do, until she caught *Madame's* probing eye through the glass just behind her, and walked off down the street. She might as well go back to Les Forêts, but somehow the thought of returning to its silent rooms alone disturbed her.

She sighed. If only Raoul were here. The last couple of weeks she had become so dependent on his presence, that with him away today on business she now felt utterly bereft, as though a necessary part of her was somehow missing . . . She realised she was staring, as though mesmerised, into a window full of fishermen's equipment, and moved on hurriedly. So that was what love did for you, she thought with a rueful grin; made you moon about over sea boots and hurricane lamps.

All the same, if only she could have gone with him, that faintly uneasy ache might have vanished. Almost wistfully, she had asked him that morning, as he was counting out hundred-franc notes for her with dizzying speed, after she had refused his charge card, but he had only dropped his usual, very correct, light kiss on her forehead, reminded her of her hair apppointment, adding that in any case she would be bored in Vannes, that he might very well be late, and besides, she needed a restful day. At the unspoken meaning in his grey eyes, she had blushed peony pink and given in . . .

She turned into the bustling main street, crowded now with lunch-time shoppers carrying bags loaded down with *baguettes* and clinking bottles. People were disgorging from every shop, and in the doorways of the department stores the security guards were waiting to close up for the long midday break. Jenni slowed, still unsure over what to do, then backed up against a shop window out of the purposeful current of bodies.

Almost opposite was an exclusive, Breton-style restaurant, where Raoul had taken her for lunch the previous week. She could go there, she supposed, but then quailed at the mere thought of eating alone, with waiters hovering solicitously over her.

And then, quite suddenly, she saw him. Raoul was on the other side of the road, still quite a distance away, but unmistakable. He must have completed his business in Vannes earlier than he had expected, and come to meet her. Jenni's heart lifted with a breathless joy, the intensity of which took her quite by surprise.

Jostled by crowds she did not even see, she pushed her way through, then waited impatiently at the pavement edge for a stream of traffic. Raoul was nearer now and he was waving to her. The cars slowed and she darted through them, waving back to him. But then, as she reached the far pavement, her hand dropped to her side and she stood motionless.

The woman whom Raoul was greeting was very chic, with a hard, polished sophistication, which turned Jenni instantaneously back into a gawky teenager. Tall, slim, thick blonde bob, a silk dress in a vibrant, paint-splash print, pencil heels. Jenni had seen her only once before, and then fleetingly, but she recognised her instantly. It was the woman from the ferry.

They were very near her now, and she shrank behind her sunglasses, shielding herself from them with passers-by—not that she need worry in the slightest, she thought with angry pain, they were as oblivious to her as to everyone.

'Raoul, *chéri*.' A husky, seductive voice.

'Hélène.'

Hélène! 'Besides, there is Hélène Marquand . . .' The girl's voice, heavy with innuendo, rang remorselessly in Jenni's ears. Of course, who else would she have been? The woman was almost as tall as Raoul, she noted automatically, so that he hardly had to incline his head to kiss her, before putting his arm lightly around her waist to guide her into the restaurant. The heavy plate door closed behind them with a soft, inexorable thud.

Jenni realised that she was clutching the strap of her shoulder-bag until her nails dug into the soft leather. She roused herself with a tremendous effort; if she continued to stand there, they might see her through the window. Very slowly, she turned and began to walk away down the street, her eyes wide but unseeing, as though sleep-walking, aware, yet careless of the curious looks she received.

When she reached the van, she let herself into it and sat quite still for a long time, gazing at nothing, before driving back, a journey of which she could not afterwards recall the slightest detail.

Somehow, she evaded the housekeeper and retreated to her turret bedroom. Uncaring of her new hairstyle, she dragged off her dress then showered, scrubbing herself violently to cleanse herself of a contamination which all the while she knew was in her mind, not her body. But the cool, soothing water had, in the end, some effect. It woke her from her numb stupor—and awoke also her innate common sense.

She went back into the bedroom and blotted herself dry, then dropped the towel and studied herself in the narrow mirror, set between two lancet windows, carefully and impartially, as though noting the finer details in the body of a total stranger. Mirror, mirror on the wall, who is the fairest of us all? She too was tall, slim, and over the last couple of weeks she had put on a little weight, so that her breasts were more rounded, the curving hipline more feminine. Suntanned, her hair glossy, she glowed with youth and vitality. But maybe, for a sophisticated man like Raoul, all that was not enough: chic sophistication, a pair of beautiful cool eyes, a husky, sensual voice, more potent . . .

Oh, for heaven's sake! She scowled at her reflection. Raoul was marrying her, wasn't he? If he'd wanted to, he could surely have married Hélène years ago. She was being the naïve child that he was always calling her. She had jumped to entirely the wrong conclusion, and on very flimsy evidence. A kiss? Well, the French were kissing each other all the time, weren't they? Just two minutes before she had seen Raoul, two beefy fishermen had fallen into each other's arms, kissing enthusiastically on both cheeks. 'Raoul, *chéri*'—well, all right, Hélène was an old friend. That waitress was what—fifteen? Her hints had been the insinuations of a young girl's salacious imagination.

And, now that she thought about it carefully, although she had accepted his words that morning as meaning that he would be in Vannes all day, he had not actually said that. What a fool she'd been. She should have gone straight up to them, instead of slinking away into the undergrowth. On the other hand . . . her cheeks burned at the thought of what Raoul might have said if she had confronted them, jealousy oozing from every pore. It would merely have confirmed his opinion of her, and then he would never, *ever* stop calling her '*ma petite*' in that casual way.

Another possibility struck her. Perhaps Hélène was a business acquaintance, and it was nothing more sinister than a working lunch. Yes, one way or the other, she had completely misinterpreted the encounter, which surely had an entirely innocent explanation that Raoul would be able to give her as soon as he came home.

In the meantime, how was she going to pass away the interminable afternoon? All the preparations for the next day were complete—most of them had been taken out of her hands, anyway. She did not even have to get ready for going away after the reception. Raoul had said that with the wedding so soon and with several business matters relating to the estate coming to a head, it would be better to postpone their honeymoon until the autumn when, he promised, he would take her to the French West Indies, or, he had added, dropping a kiss on the tip of her nose, anywhere else she chose. Jenni had not minded at all. Everything had rushed upon her lately with the speed of an express train, so that she was relieved rather than otherwise. It would also give her a chance to draw breath, to settle in to her exciting and completely new way of life.

The house was at the same time both empty and stifling, and she felt all at once that she must get outside. As she fished out from the wardrobe a pair of jeans and a loose white blouse, she caught sight of a tissue-shrouded shape at the far end, and for a moment her heart contracted painfully with a mixture of expectation and apprehension. It was a very simple, long white silk dress, to be crowned with a tiny coronet of seed pearls and silk rosebuds—her wedding gown, which she would wear to marry Raoul . . . She smiled, and the smile was still lingering as she went lightly down the turret staircase.

It was several hours before she returned, having sat beside the lake, idly tossing pebbles into the dark water with the superstitious feeling that she must make absolutely certain that Raoul would be there when she got back. But in the dining-room one place only was laid, and when the maid brought in her soup she told Jenni that he had telephoned to say that he would be late and would not require dinner.

All her nebulous fears and suspicions rekindled into vivid, explosive life. She forced herself to go through some semblance of eating, trying to evade the cool pair of eyes in her grandmother's portrait on the wall opposite her, but as soon as the maid had finally withdrawn she carried the coffee-tray into the sitting-room. She switched on the television, but every channel seemed to have an incomprehensible soap opera or an interminable *actualités* bulletin, and in the end she gave up and, for some reason she could not—or would not—understand, heaved Igor's basket through from the kitchen, then sat, abstractedly fondling his head as the delicate gilt clock on the mantelpiece remorselessly tinkled the quarter hours until she could have thrown it against the wall.

As it grew dark she went across to close the curtains, but then stood staring out into the dusk, instead, the lighted room behind her, until at last she went slowly back to the sofa. A terrible, chill sensation of loneliness, of isolation, was taking hold of her mind. The realisation forced itself upon her, as never before, that she was in a strange country, in a strange house, surrounded totally by strangers; even Raoul, she thought with a sudden twist of panic, seemed to her at this moment a frightening stranger. There was no one she could talk to, no one she could turn to, confide in; even Claudette, like everyone else, now treated her in a subtly different way, her natural warmth tinged with a certain wariness.

Raoul had insisted on her writing formally to her stepfather to invite him to the wedding, but in her letter she had foolishly omitted, she thought ironically, to mention that her future husband was a wealthy landowner, her home a château, and so, not surprisingly, he had not even written to acknowledge the invitation. And yet, she thought suddenly, tears filling her eyes, if he and Sue were to walk in at that moment, she would be hard put to it not to fling her arms round both of them.

Eleven o'clock. Perhaps Raoul was not even coming back
tonight. Perhaps he was intending to go, she thought, with a
new cynicism, straight from the arms of his mistress to the
ceremony. Perhaps at this very moment they were . . . At the
picture her thoughts conjured up in her mind, she almost
gasped aloud as a spasm of physical anguish wrenched her
body. Her childish, romantic idea of love was wrong,
hopelessly wrong. Love, after all, was this terrible, destructive
pain which made her want to lash out, to wound as she had
been wounded. She closed her eyes and began rocking herself
back and forth to try to assuage the misery . . .

'Wake up, Jenni.'

Her mind blurred with sleep, she stared up at Raoul, who
was jacketless, his tie loosened, the top buttons of his cream
shirt open. He smiled down at her and squatted beside her.

'I am flattered. You could not go to bed without seeing me,
but, *ma petite,* you should be in your room and fast asleep
now. It is after midnight.'

He leaned forward to kiss her, but as he did so she smelled
the faint sweetness of wine on his breath and saw—or, at least,
thought she saw—a smug gleam of male triumph in his eyes.

'Don't you touch me!'

She jerked away from him and huddled into the far corner of
the sofa, pressing her body against the soft leather. Raoul sat
back on his haunches, his dark brows drawing down in a
frown.

'What folly is this?'

For once impervious to his threatening expression, she said
coldly, 'I trust you had a—satisfactory time in Vannes?'

Raoul stared at her, his eyes narrowing. 'Yes, I did. It was a
thoroughly satisfactory meeting.'

'I'm so glad.'

She wanted desperately to throw herself at him, to sob all her fears out in his arms, but she must not allow herself to do that, so instead she said, with all the haughtiness she could muster, 'And I'm sure you particularly enjoyed your lunch.' Overriding Raoul's attempted interruption, she went on hurriedly, 'It must have been quite some meal to last until midnight.' Her throat was so tight now that she could hardly speak. 'I suppose you could say it was lunch with all the trimmings!'

This barb struck her as being so witty that she began to laugh, and she went on laughing until he seized her by the shoulders and shook her hard. The laugh died away on a hiccup then, and he released his hold on her, throwing himself down in the chair opposite. Even now, she thought, it was not too late. All he needed to say was, look, Jenni, I am sorry, I know I should not have seen her the day before our wedding, but——

'And now, perhaps,' his voice was icy, that curving, sensual mouth a thin line, 'you will be good enough to explain this—this exhibition.'

'You c-couldn't even keep away from her today, could you?'

'Who?' His voice was even colder, and there was a definite warning note in it, but she recklessly ignored it.

'Hélène Marquand, of course—who else?'

A dull red flush, which boded ill for someone, rose on Raoul's cheekbones. 'Who has been talking to you? I demand that you tell me.'

Jenni quailed inwardly at the flash of anger in his metallic grey eyes, but somehow forced an insouciant shrug. 'No one. I'm not stupid, whatever you might think, and I've just been doing my sums correctly. You know, adding two and two and making four. You and she——'

'Be silent, or you will say something you will have cause to regret.' His voice, though low, stopped her dead. 'You have been making, as you so elegantly put it, a great deal more than four. No—let me finish. I have not, as you obviously imagine, just torn myself away from Hélène's lovely body.' She winced at his words, but he went on remorselessly, 'I have, in fact, spent the evening in the company of not one, but two highly attractive women, although their husbands, both very old friends of mine, were also with us. I hope you do not object?'

She flinched at the heavy sarcasm in his voice, as he went on, 'As for Hélène . . .' He paused for a moment, eyeing her thoughtfully. 'You may—thanks to me—have the immediate trappings of sophistication, but underneath you have shown yourself to be still a foolish child. But you have to grow up, and you may as well begin now. I am nearly thirty-three years old. I was not aware that Les Forêts was a monastery, even if, from your shocked expression, you consider that I should have lived in it like some neutered monk.'

He uncoiled himself and, before she could move a muscle, dropped on to the sofa beside her. He put his hand under her chin, tilting her face to meet his eyes. 'You guessed rightly, in one respect at least. Hélène was my mistress. She is three years older than me, but she is a very beautiful, sensual woman—but then, you will have noticed that for yourself, no doubt. And no, it was not some squalid, underhand intrigue. She lived with me here quite openly for some time.'

She had lived here with Raoul, actually lived here, in this apartment? Jenni swallowed down a feeling of choking nausea. Sat beside him on this sofa, eaten with him in the dining-room, and shared his—— She closed her eyes against the tide of jealousy that was welling up inside her, bringing horrible images that she did not want to see. With one small part of her mind she knew that she was being irrational, childishly so. And yet, the thought of them both here, in such—loving intimacy filled her with grey misery.

'But it ended some time ago, by mutual agreement. She herself is married, of course—to a wealthy art dealer, and now she spends most of her time, not down here, but in Paris. But we have remained friends. In France, we can be very—civilised about such matters. Just a few weeks ago, when she was visiting England and I was going to Roscoff on business——' He broke off abruptly. 'But, of course, that is when you will have first seen her. She rang me yesterday, to send her best wishes for our future happiness,' his voice was tinged with irony, 'and to ask if we could meet for lunch. I did not think it necessary—or perhaps advisable—to inform you. But I repeat, our affair had ended before you came to Les Forêts.'

Jenni turned her head away. Raoul, she knew, was not trying to deceive her, and yet, whatever he might believe—*she* had seen the way Hélène had looked at him, feasting her eyes on him greedily, a terrible hunger in them, which only Jenni, loving him so desperately herself, could recognise. Hélène had perhaps, for pride's sake, pretended that she too was weary of their liaison, but it was Raoul, and he alone, Jenni knew intuitively, who had ended their affair. This should, she reflected, have made her feel quite secure, but somehow it only served to heighten her uneasiness . . .

If Raoul had tired of this sophisticated, lovely woman, how could *she* hope to retain his love—if indeed she had ever truly had it? Perhaps her unaffected innocence, and—yes, she told herself savagely, her very immaturity—the contrast she must have presented to Hélène had held a certain attraction for him. Surely, though, this could be no more than a passing fancy and

—her eyes darkened with pain—he would all too soon realise that behind her inexperience she had nothing to offer him. In the future there would doubtless be, if not Hélène herself, many other Hélènes, and she would not be able to bear that.

When she had accepted his proposal, she had vowed to make him forget all other women, but she had fooled herself. She would never be able to do that, and in the end, she thought, with a kind of dreary hopelessness, she would be forced to settle for the aching sadness of an empty marriage, all the time fearful of any attractive woman who might stray into Raoul's path. And so——

'I—I'm not going through with it.' There was a hair's breadth silence, then she added, just in case he had not understood her, 'The wedding, I mean.'

Raoul gave a harsh laugh. 'Well, I did gather that that was what you meant. But, *chérie*, I am afraid that you are quite mistaken. You *will* marry me. I will not face public ridicule over the delicate niceties of a schoolchild!' The contempt in his tone was undisguised. 'And, *enfin*, what do you imagine that you will do? You will doubtless wish to keep a close eye on your inheritance.' All the former anger was crackling in his voice. 'So do you intend to stay on in the château, in the face of humiliation? *D'ailleurs*, can you not imagine the scandal if you remain under the same roof as myself? Or will you perhaps return to England, to your stepfather——'

He broke off as though waiting for some response, but Jenni, who had been sitting, head bent, could only look up at him, in mute appeal for him not to go on. For a fleeting second, she almost—almost thought there was a flicker of compassion in those hard grey eyes, but when he continued, it was to say, '—the man who is so caring of you that he will not even attend your wedding?'

Jenni leaped to her feet precipitately and went over to the

mantelpiece. She stood with her back to him, pressing her
knuckles to her mouth, and closed her eyes momentarily.
This, the man she had naïvely believed must love her, was
now coldly, remorselessly flaying her alive, inflicting a wound
on her with every syllable. But somehow she must not let him
see how he was annihilating her. She drew in an unsteady
breath, then very slowly turned to him, her face colourless.

'I see it all now. You're quite right—I am a fool,' she said
tonelessly. How often had he called her a child? And then,
tonight, he had told her she must grow up. Well, she was
doing that very rapidly now—years by the minute. 'I thought
you——' she broke off, fighting to control the trembling of her
mouth '—but you only want to marry me to get your hands on
the whole estate. That was why you s-seduced me.'

The lamps around the room were sprouting blurred, golden
haloes, and she blinked away the moistness, then went on, her
voice dulled by a weary desolation, 'You were afraid that I
might marry someone else, and then, if my husband proved to
be tougher than you,' though such a prospect was quite
impossible: no one—no one was as hard and ruthless as this
man, 'you might have had a fight on your hands to keep full
control of the estate.'

Raoul's fists tensed on the edge of the sofa, and for a
moment she thought he was going to leap up and violently
seize hold of her. To Jenni, numbed by misery, such an assault
would have been almost a welcome relief from her pent-up
anguish, but then he relaxed back again, merely giving a brief,
contemptuous shrug.

'If that is what you choose to believe, *ma chère*, then that is
your concern. But, Eugénie Aimée Kerouac,' there was a cold
implacability in every line of his face, a harder edge to his voice
than she had ever heard before, 'you will be ready in just——'
he glanced at his watch '—eight hours' time to accompany me

to the *mairie* for the civil ceremony, and then, at midday, you will be in the church, wearing the dress *I* have bought for you, to receive the ring which *I* shall put on your finger.'

For a long moment he held Jenni's gaze, then she turned away, her shoulders sagging. She would obey him, of course, and he knew it. There was no need for him to spell it out for her. She could not remain in Brittany unless she married him—Raoul would somehow see to that—and in England there was no job, no home, no family, nothing.

She shook her head, tumbling her hair forward to hide her face, then walked slowly across to the door, her legs dragging as though the floor were a clinging mire. She felt his eyes burning on her back, but he did not prevent her leaving; and when, in the doorway, she half turned towards him, he was leaning back, his stormy eyes fixed moodily on the carpet at his feet.

As she closed the door behind her and leaned her head for a few moments agaisnt the cool panel, she heard the little carriage clock strike. One o'clock. Her wedding day. What was that old superstition? She gave a shaky laugh, which changed half-way to a strangled sob. Surely people said, didn't they, that for the bride and groom to meet before the ceremony was an omen of ill fortune?

CHAPTER TEN

THE WEDDING day passed with a grim inexorability, a kaleidoscope of tiny, painful cameos . . . Madame Cherbay fussing into her room with a breakfast tray, which Jenni pushed away virtually untasted . . . showering and putting on, like some dazed automaton, the elegantly simple dress of pale beige linen, with tiny brown and black polka-dots, and straw boater with its matching band . . . Raoul, darkly handsome in his pale grey morning-suit, waiting for her in the entrance hall of the château . . . raising her hand to his lips, the secret, sardonic gleam in his eyes for her alone . . . the drive, mercifully short, to the *mairie* for the brief, impersonal civil ceremony . . .

. . . Stepping into the shimmering folds of white silk, as the young *coiffeuse* rhapsodised over *'une si belle mariée'*, although Jenni herself saw only a slim, pale ghost, shadows smudged under its eyes . . . François David arriving to escort her to the village church, taking one of her hands in his with a funny, half-sad smile, and kissing it, so that she almost broke down on the spot and wept into his elegant, pale waistcoat . . . the simple service, heart-achingly beautiful, yet fleeting . . . Raoul, frowning slightly as he slid the ring down over her knuckle . . . then, in her turn, *'au nom du Père, du Fils et . . .'* her cold hands trembling as she put the broad circlet of gold on his finger, so that in the end he had to help her, before his lips brushed hers in a formal, chaste kiss . . .

. . . Then, the return to the château, Raoul's protecting

arm guiding her through a shower of orange and rose
blossoms from the estate staff lined up on the steps outside
. . . the darkly panelled *salle*, now brilliant with light from
the crystal chandeliers, and under them the long, oval
rosewood dining-table, set for the elaborate wedding
breakfast, she at one end, as hostess, and Raoul, urbane yet
always watchful, at the far end . . . laughter, voices raised in
lively conversation, as one delicious course after another
was presented by white-gloved waiters . . . champagne,
endless champagne—no other wine—although she merely
moistened her dry lips from time to time as the bubbles
faded . . . smiling, perpetually smiling, until her jaw ached
from tension, at François David and his vivacious wife,
seated on either side of her . . . and always, it seemed, a pair
of coolly thoughtful grey eyes on her . . .

. . . The small, perfect, white and gold ballroom, the
prettiest room in the château, where the guests mingled
with estate workers and villagers, and where, to smiling
applause, Raoul made her a grave half-bow and led her out
to dance an old-fashioned waltz. He had drunk a great
deal—she had surreptitiously noticed that—but there was
only a faint flush over his cheekbones, and his eyes were
steady, although the expression in them was one which
deeply disturbed her.

He gave her an intensely loving look and said, very softly,
'Smile, *ma petite*, and do me the honour, please, of
endeavouring to look a little less like an early martyr staring
at an arena full of lions.'

Jenni gave him one startled look, then somehow forced a
stiff smile, for the benefit of François David and his wife,
who were almost at their elbow. At the same time, she
allowed Raoul to draw her closer, so that she was all at once
acutely aware of the taut lines of his body.

At last, the interminable dance ended and he escorted her back to her seat; then, as her eyes followed him, he went over to claim Claudette, nervously fluttering, for the next dance. Jenni watched as he whirled her round, smiling warmly down at her, until she visibly relaxed, even glowed in his arms . . .

The impeccably mannered host, Raoul talked, danced, laughed among the guests, and somehow she also laughed, danced, even sparkled, but with a vivacity which she knew to be totally hollow. It was, she thought, as though two parallel scenes were running. In the room, all around her, it was warmth, colour, music, gaiety; while she, the focus of it all, was a mere spectator, as chill eddies of fear and apprehension swirled about her . . .

And then, the moment she had endeavoured to prepare herself for all day, but still she paled and went rigid as Raoul's arm encircled her waist, and the pressure of his fingers, light enough to an onlooker, but in reality as inexorable as steel, drew her inconspicuously away; away from the lights, the music, the friendly faces, the security . . .

He closed the ballroom door and leaned against it, his grey eyes watching her.

'*Eh bien*, my lovely wife, are you not going to say, "At last, my beloved husband, we are alone"?' His voice was lightly mocking, but there was an undercurrent, a something, which made her shiver for a moment. 'Or is it precisely that thought which is putting such an unbecoming crease between your brows?'

He reached out and softly brushed across her forehead with his fingers, his touch sending tiny shock-waves through her. Then, before she could react, he took her hand and led her off down the corridor, the noises behind them

dying away until their footsteps, echoing on the marble
flags, were the only sound.

When they reached the door leading to his apartment, he
opened it, gestured her through, then, as she stood, her
fingers twisting in an endless cat's cradle, locked it from the
inside. He pushed the sitting-room door open and she went
in, Igor pattering behind her. Someone, Madame Cherbay
presumably, had fastened a huge white satin bow to his
collar, which now hung lopsidedly under his chin, so Jenni
automatically bent to straighten it, then suddenly hugged
him to her violently until he gave a muffled yelp of protest
and wriggled free.

Raoul came in, jacketless, carrying a bottle of white wine
and two glasses. In silence, he poured two generous glasses
and handed her one.

'You drank nothing with the meal—such an appalling
waste of vintage champagne—so please join me now in our
own private toast.'

He pulled off his tie and eased open the stiff white shirt
by a couple of buttons, then threw himself down on the sofa
beside her, his leg trapping a fold of white silk, so that she
could not edge further away from him.

'Now, Jenni, what do you suggest we drink to?'

Her eyes met his for a moment, but then flinched away
from the sardonic glint in them. Nervously, one finger
carefully encircling the rim of the icy glass, she murmured,
'I—I don't know.'

'Well, then—to our future. To the Kerouac inheritance.'
There was no mistaking the undertone of irony in his voice.

Like an obedient puppet, she raised her glass to click it
against his, then took a tentative sip of the pale gold liquid.
Summer was in it, the scent of flowers and meadows warm
under the sun, and suddenly there arose from the glass,

almost like a perfume, the memory of a June morning, of
hawthorn and of haygrass white with dew . . . Her eyes
brimmed momentarily with tears, which she forced back
before he could become aware of them.

'I hope you approve of our wine.' And as she looked at
him questioningly, he went on, 'Oh, yes, it is a Kerouac
Sauterne. 1971—*une grande année*, laid down for just such
an occasion as this.'

As he drank, she shot him a lightning glance, but he was
leaning back, relaxed and, she saw now, with a little spurt of
resentment, totally at ease. But after all, there was no reason
why he should not be; this was his territory, she the newcomer. And besides, he had got his way, hadn't he? She had
not thwarted him, had not refused to marry him, so that he
no doubt, even as he had slipped this wide gold band on her
finger, had been privately congratulating himself that his
intention to make himself total master of Les Forêts had
come a little nearer . . . 'What I have, I hold on to . . .' Well,
she too was in his hands now, another of his possessions,
that necessary legal encumbrance.

With a sudden, unsteady movement, she lifted the glass
to her lips and drained it. Raoul took it from between her
fingers and set it down on the table. He straightened up and
lifted her to her feet, giving her a faint, ambivalent smile.
There was though, she thought, no anger in him, as though
the harrowing scene of the previous evening, enacted in this
very room, had been completely obliterated from his mind.

'Go through to the bedroom, *ma petite*. I will get rid of
these glasses.'

Well, Madame Cherbay had certainly tried her hardest
with the room, Jenni thought involuntarily, as she stared
around her a few moments later. Vases filled with flowers
from the gardens and more exotic blooms from the

conservatory stood on every surface, the air was heavy with
their mingled scents, while the darkly severe bedspread had
been replaced by a heavy white honeycomb counterpane,
folded down to reveal peach-coloured bedlinen, and
peeping from under a pillow was, though she averted her
eyes hastily, one of her trousseau nightdresses, bought of
course by Raoul. Somehow, though, the room remained
inviolate: totally masculine, wholly uncompromising,
exactly like its owner. She stood fingering a bowl of
delicately trumpeted yellow freesia.

'*Dieu!* I see now what Madame meant.' Raoul was behind
her in the doorway and she did not turn. 'She feared that
you might find this room too like your grandmother's.'
Then, as she forced herself to turn slowly to him, he added,
'Rather overpowering, that is. And she asked, therefore, if
she could add a few softening—feminine touches.' He
grimaced. 'It might, on the whole, have been simpler if we
had spent our wedding night out in the conservatory, *n'est-
ce pas?* But it pleases you, at least?'

Jenni looked away from him abruptly once more. 'Y-yes,
it's very pretty.' She had hardly spoken a word since leaving
the reception, and now her voice seemed oddly husky.

'Good. I shall tell her so.'

He had crossed the thick carpet soundlessly, and she
tensed up in every muscle as she felt his breath stirring the
tendrils of soft hair on her neck. She jumped violently as his
hands moved to her shoulders.

'Relax, Jenni.' His voice was soothing—almost, she
thought, as though he were calming a nervous child. 'Do
not shy from me like a highly strung thoroughbred. You
cannot possibly manage these buttons on your dress. Have I
told you, by the way, how beautiful you have looked today?'

Jenny mumbled something inaudible, then forced herself

to stand motionless as his fingers moved slowly down the curve of her back, carefully unhooking each tiny, silk-covered button. Once his skin brushed against hers, evoking an involuntary shiver from her, but Raoul did not seem to notice. He eased the dress gently away from her shoulders.

'There. And now,' his voice was quite matter of fact, 'you will want to wash away the tensions of the day. Do you wish to bathe first?'

'Oh, no, it's quite all right. You can go first,' Jenni said, still in that odd, breathless voice. She felt that she must have a little while on her own, to prepare herself . . .

Raoul shrugged, then slid open a wardrobe door, hung up his jacket, unhooked a navy robe and went through to the bathroom, closing the door behind him.

But he might come back at any moment . . . Jenni pulled down the wedding dress, seeing without pleasure its pearly folds foaming round her feet. Almost trembling, she tossed it aside, then fumbled through the drawers which she knew were now full of her underwear . . .

When Raoul, his dark hair still glistening damp from the shower, returned a short while later, she was perched on the extreme edge of the bed, wearing not her trousseau négligé, but her old cotton housecoat. He raised his brows expressively at the sight of it, but said nothing and she, gathering up the nightdress like a bundle of old rags under one arm, fled past him, all too aware that under the dark robe his strong, tanned body was naked.

She banged the bathroom door to, and as she leaned against it for support, caught sight of herself in one of the mirrors, her eyes huge and fixed, like some hunted animal's. She moved hastily away from the door and sat on the rim of the bath, staring instead at the ivory-coloured embossed tiles, and worrying at her lower lip with her

teeth. What on earth was wrong with her? Wedding-night
jitters? But that was ridiculous. Raoul had already made
love to her, on that magic far-away morning in the barn,
with may blossom in her hair, and buttercup pollen on her
feet, made love tenderly, gently, cradling her lovingly in his
arms. Lovingly. She frowned slightly, her hazel eyes
darkening. Perhaps that was it. Innocent girl that she had
been, she had thought—well, all right, persuaded herself,
she thought with a whiplash of self-impatience—that he
loved her. Now, of course, she knew better, didn't she? But
in the meantime, Raoul, practised and skilful as he had
shown himself to be, was waiting for her . . . She flung the
delicate wisp of amber and cream silk lace on to the floor
and undressed for her shower.

When she eventually returned to the bedroom Raoul was
leaning against the window-frame, staring out into the
summer twilight. He half turned as she came in hesitantly,
then with a swift movement drew the heavy curtains across,
plunging the room into the soft light of one bedside lamp.
He stood looking at her without speaking, slowly surveying
her body, only half hidden by the translucent, filmy lace, so
that she put her hand up instinctively to her throat, at the
new, deeply disturbing expression in his eyes. He had not
looked at her like this even on that morning, and now, when
he crossed the room to her, she closed her eyes involuntarily
against the spiral, half panic, half unwilling desire, which
was uncoiling itself insidiously inside her like a serpent.

But he only said, 'Let me help you,' and she felt his hands
slowly unpinning the head-dress which she, in her abstrac-
tion, had totally forgotten about. He removed all the pins at
last, then carelessly threw the pretty coronet down on the
dressing-table, while with his other hand he lifted her hair
free, so that it fell round her face in a gleaming wave.

The pull of his hand on hers was gentle but quite irresistible, as he led her over to the bed. But Jenni kept her hand rigid, for fear that the pulse that was beating suffocatingly through her whole body now would betray her to him, and she must not allow that. After all, this was not a marriage of love; Raoul had never hinted that he loved her. No, it was a marriage of convenience that she, so desperate for love, had allowed herself to be ensnared into—to do no more than neatly shackle together two disparate halves, both of them, in their different ways, victims of an old woman's dying whim. But she was now, irrevocably, Raoul's wife, to be regarded by him, and by the world, as his property, his possession . . .

He laid her back against the pillow, then leaned towards her, resting his hands on each side of her so that she was trapped between them. His kiss was soft and undemanding, but then his lips slowly slid down her throat, lingering over the pulse in the hollow at the base, then on over the swell of her half-revealed breast. He lowered himself on one elbow and with his free hand eased the lace strap down from her shoulder and cupped her breast, his fingers stroking gently across its aroused centre, so that at last she gave a faint, unsteady sigh.

'Do I please you, *ma petite?*'

His eyes, very near, were searching, and she could only nod helplessly and whisper, 'You know you do.'

But then she saw a fleeting half-smile cross his lips, and all at once the spell of sensuous magic that he had created was shattered. It was the smile, she thought with sudden jarring conviction, of an experienced lover, long skilled in the arts of wooing seduction and confident of success. So he had smiled at other women—and at one woman in particular. Jenni had a sudden, violently repellent image of

Hélène, smiling a sleek cat's smile of lazy contentment here, in this bed where she was lying now, and in sickening revulsion she put up both her hands to thrust him away from her.

'Don't touch me! Leave me alone!'

She rolled away from him, shuddering, but he pulled her back towards him. She stared up at him blindly, the contorted, intertwined images of Raoul and Hélène flickering through her brain so that she could hardly see him.

He expelled his breath in an angry hiss and gave her arm a shake.

'What *bêtise* is this?'

'I've told you,' she said, forcing her voice, by a supreme effort, to remain steady. 'Leave me alone. I don't want you to make love to me.'

He gave a short, angry laugh. 'But, *chérie*, I received a distinctly different impression from you just a few moments ago. And even now——'his eyes raked insolently down over her flushed cheeks, her breasts, still taut '—your body tells me the truth, even if you choose to lie to me.'

He leaned across and, catching her by the arms, roughly pulled her towards him, but when she cried out in terror he only said grimly, 'Do not be afraid, *ma chère*. I have told you before, I have never yet had to take a woman by force, and I have no wish to start with my wife. But,' he drew her even closer to him, so that their eyes were only inches apart, 'unless you wish to sit here, in this uncomfortable posture until morning, tell me what you mean.'

Jenni gazed into his angry face, those grey eyes, which had once held such a tenderness that she could almost have believed . . . She swallowed, then said, 'If you must know, it's—it's that I keep thinking of all the other women there have no doubt been——'

He gave a half-smothered exclamation. 'You make it sound as though I had some sort of permanent harem established in here!' He stared at her intently, then went on slowly, his eyes narrowing, 'But it is not all those other women, as your prim little mouth put it—it is *one* woman, is it not? It is Hélène Marquand.' He gave a coldly derisory smile. 'You are jealous of her, of an affair which I have told you is over. What a baby you are.'

'Oh!' She gave a gasp of outrage. How could he say that? He should understand, surely, how she must feel about—that woman. Of course it wasn't jealousy, it was just that the mere thought of them together here in this room, in this bed . . .

She forced herself to set her chin defiantly. 'I'm not jealous. After all, why should I be?' She gave him a careless smile. 'If I loved you, I might be jealous, but as it is, well——' She shrugged.

Raoul's fingers tightened on her arm in a painful grip, then he slowly relaxed his hold, and his arms fell to his side.

'Well, well,' he said slowly, 'I said that you were a talented actress. Perhaps you are an even better one than I had suspected. That morning in the *gîte*, and when I asked you to marry me——' He broke off abruptly, his lips tightening. 'But perhaps, after all, it was merely a means to an end for you.'

He stared at her, an odd, unreadable expression in his eyes, until Jenni wilted under his gaze; then he got up, loosening the belt of his robe.

'W—what are you doing?' she faltered.

He gave a bitter laugh. 'Oh, do not disturb yourself. I assure you I have no intention of—harming you further.'

She turned her eyes away hastily as he peeled off the robe
and threw it across a chair. 'I am going to sleep.'

He pulled back the covers and slid down into the bed. A
moment later the light was extinguished, and she heard him
turn on to his side, away from her, as though
contemptuously dismissing her from his mind. She,
though, sat still for a few moments, her anger evaporating
until she felt only a dull, barren misery.

Then she too slipped gingerly down into the bed, as far
from Raoul as she could, though he made no sign whatever
that he was aware of her. She lay motionless in the warm
darkness until she was sure that he was asleep, and only
then did the tear which had been threatening for so long roll
down the curve of her cheek to lose itself in the pillow. She
was still crying soundlessly when at last she too slept.

CHAPTER ELEVEN

IN THE DAYS and nights which followed, Jenni tormented herself with one thought. If only she had woken earlier that first morning, perhaps—perhaps it would not have been too late, and then this terrible, aching misery would have been assuaged. But when she roused, Raoul was already dressed; he was wearing one of the casual denim suits he used for work, beige, with a fine-knit black shirt.

She heard him pick up his keys, then watched through almost closed eyelids as he stood by the dressing-table for a moment, tapping his fingers, as though irresolute. She lay, her breathing suspended between fear and excitement, as he looked towards her, but then he turned away abruptly and left the room, softly closing the door behind him, and a few minutes later she heard him speaking to Madame Cherbay.

When Jenni forced herself to appear an hour or so later, she cringed inwardly at the thought that the housekeeper might register some faint surprise that on the very morning after their wedding Raoul was behaving exactly as usual. However, Madame and the maid, who served her breakfast in the dining-room, were either too well schooled to show any such emotion or too accustomed to Raoul's dynamism to see anything even faintly odd in it; rather the latter, she suspected, with intense relief . . .

And that had become the pattern of their lives. Raoul would remain in the sitting-room every evening, long after she had retired, drinking a great deal, she was certain. She struggled

continually to tear the paralysing fear from her mind which
she knew was destroying her marriage before it had even
begun, but although she knew that he was right, that she
was being ridiculously childish, she still could not exorcise
Hélène's malevolent spirit, which haunted every corner of
the apartment.

Consequently, she fought against making any move
towards him, terrified that Hélène would come between
them once again. She had even, after that first night,
pushed the beautiful nightdress into the back of a drawer,
well out of sight, and worn instead her old cotton ones. But
then, each night, she had thought bleakly that she need not
have bothered, for Raoul got into bed, turned on his side
away from her, with the briefest of goodnights, for all the
world as though that invisible sword of chastity still lay
between them, and dropped straight into a seemingly
untroubled sleep, leaving her to toss restlessly until the
early hours.

Each morning when she woke, the space beside her was
empty, only a faint indentation in the pillow and a faint
warmth when she rolled over to his side of the bed betrayed
that he had slept beside her. If she had not been fearful of
the staff, she would, she told herself wearily one morning,
as she sat up in bed pressing her cheek to his pillow, have
given up the whole dreadful charade and moved back to the
child's turret bedroom.

Raoul was always scrupulously polite, even imbuing his
voice with a spurious warmth when one of the servants was
within earshot, and then she would hear her own voice,
responding with a forced lightness which set her very teeth
on edge. One evening, though, he arrived very late for
dinner, and sat, even more preoccupied than usual,
frowning abstractedly over his plate. Then Jenni, directly

under the chilly gaze of her grandmother's portrait, crumbled her bread into a heap of tiny rubber balls as she watched their reflections in the huge gilt mirror and wondered, with a detached misery, how many other unhappy couples it had reflected, sitting silently at this polished rosewood table, and whether for ever this was to be the pattern of their lives.

Suddenly, she had an almost irresistible urge to leap to her feet, screaming, and hurl every piece of fine china, every glass and every silver knife and fork, into the mirror—or better still at Raoul's unconscious head. But, even as her hand began to curve itself of its own volition around the delicate crystal stem of her wine glass, the maid came in with dishes of crème caramel . . .

And he had even slapped down her timorous offers of help, she thought resentfully. Remembering a country house near her stepfather's home, which had recently been beautifully refurbished by the new owner's wife, and was now drawing daily crowds of paying visitors, she had suggested something along those lines to Raoul, even that she could learn the long history of Les Forêts and show parties around herself. But he had impatiently dismissed the idea, saying that the state-rooms were fine as they were and he did not intend, in any case, that his wife would spend her days guiding endless lines of visitors around *his* house.

Again, wandering one morning from room to room in a far, unused wing of the château, it had occurred to her that, having already at some time in the past been split up into servants' quarters, the top floor could, with little expense, be made into self-contained apartments for exclusive holiday lets. But that evening, Raoul, seemingly even more self-engrossed than usual, had curtly dismissed that idea also, leaving her smarting and angry. After all, it was her estate too, wasn't it? Or was it?

There was, of course, no question of her returning to work at the camping site. She did not even bother to suggest this to Raoul, knowing how he would react to such an idea. And on the few occasions that she ventured across to the site, the subtle change in attitude towards her that she had already detected in Claudette was matched by that of the remainder of the staff, the easy camaraderie she had so briefly enjoyed being replaced by a wary formality which Jenni found almost as distressing as outright hostility would have been.

Then, one evening, Raoul had got up from the dinner-table and offhandedly informed her that he had work to do in his office. It was a lovely summer night, so instead of switching on the television as she usually did, in search of moving wallpaper to deaden her mind, Jenni went outside into the walled garden, hoping to soothe herself with the intoxicating scents of roses and lavender rising in the still, warm air.

But, as she wandered about the gravelled walks, sudden painful memories came to her of that other evening in this garden, when Raoul had verbally flayed her, taking her apart so successfully that it seemed to her that, even now, she had not managed quite to put herself together again. He had stood there, one elbow leaning against the stone sundial . . . Jenni screwed her face up suddenly as the lacerating memories revived, and went back to the terrace.

Outside the office, though, she was brought up with a start. Raoul had the desk-lamp switched on; it illuminated him, leaving the rest of the room in deep shadow. He was sitting at the desk, a pile of papers in front of him, a pen in his hand, but he was staring fixedly at the wall opposite, as though intent on memorising every line of the pattern, and something—a weariness, almost—about his half-averted face wrenched at her heart.

Hardly knowing what she was doing, she went back through the french windows and through into the office. As she entered, he looked up, his face remote and shuttered.

'I—I was just wondering——' she began, then stopped, already regretting the impulse.

'What?' His tone was far from encouraging.

'Well—I just wish you'd tell me if there's anything wrong—with the estate, I mean,' she put in hastily, 'if there's any way I can help you.'

He stared up at her for a long moment, then said, 'No. There is nothing that need concern you.'

There was a finality in his voice which chilled her. She stared down at him, then without another word turned abruptly on her heel, knowing that if she stood there a moment longer her stiff face would crumple piteously and she would have the humiliation of breaking down in front of him.

So even helping him with the estate was to be denied her—for pride demanded that she would never ask again. But, of course, should she—in his eyes, an unwanted but necessary encumbrance—have expected anything more? Once, she had been dangerous. By marrying her, he had removed the danger as you would pull the sting from a wasp, but he was none the less forced to remain shackled to her for ever. And for her part, marriage had given her nothing—no real security, no closeness, no love . . .

She went back to the sitting-room and huddled for a long time on the sofa, her arms around Igor, her head against his bony chest, both of them apparently engrossed in a film about the home life of soldier ants . . .

* * *

And then earlier this evening, in the middle of dinner, there
had been a phone call. Raoul had sprung up, almost with
alacrity, Jenni thought miserably, and returned a long time
later, looking grim and with a smouldering anger clearly
visible in his steely-grey eyes that boded very badly for
someone. He'd told her briefly that he had to leave for
Bordeaux early next morning, and meantime he intended to
spend the evening, not in his office, but out riding in the
park.

When he had gone, Jenni sat staring at her plate for a long
time. Something had clearly disturbed him, and he needed
to release the tension within him—but not by passing the
evening with her.

The delicate flowered pattern on her dessert plate blurred
all at once, and with an incoherent exclamation she pushed
back her chair and quitted the room, to drift around the
château like a wraith, through room after room of sheeted
furniture, and then out into the grounds, first stumbling
along at breakneck pace, as though fleeing something
terrible, then wandering aimlessly, almost in a stupor,
through the fields and meadows and into the woods, her
footsteps rustling among the previous autumn's dried beech
husks. At length she leaned against a tree, resting her head
against its gnarled, silvery trunk, and thought, perhaps I
won't go back—perhaps I'll never go back . . .

Just ahead of her, a group of roe deer crossed the path,
picking their way with delicate precision, then as they
scented her they scuttered away, rousing her from her
torpor. She had wandered a long way, and while she had
been in the wood the sun had set and the darkness was
deepening around her. As she stood, staring about her
stupidly, she heard a faint sound and, straining her senses,
she made out, coming slowly along the track towards her, a

horse and rider. A surge of relief engulfed her, and without stopping to consider if it was Raoul, or whether he would be even remotely pleased to see her, she darted forward.

The horse shied and pranced sideways as the rider reined it in.

'*Diable!* Jenni? What are you doing here?'

There was shocked surprise in his voice, and a frisson of something else, which she could not quite seize on. He swung himself down from the saddle and took off his riding hat, ruffling his hair.

'Oh, I—I went for a walk and got lost.' Then, as he stared intently down at her, she added, 'D—do you mind if I walk back with you—that is, if you're going back yet?'

'Not afraid of the woods of Les Forêts, surely, *ma petite?*' There was a flash of white teeth in the dusk. 'Though I must admit that the local people still whisper some strange stories. Whether they quite believe them or not, I do not know, but it is true that I have never had trouble with poachers in this part of the estate.'

He put his hand lightly on her shoulder. 'Of course I will escort you. That is—unless you feel that perhaps there is more to fear from me than from the ghosts of Isabelle and her lover,' Jenni shivered and imperceptibly drew a little nearer to him, 'as they gallop for ever in a vain attempt to save their forfeit lives.'

They left the line of woodland and crossed an open stretch of meadow above which, on a low ridge, she saw through the settling dusk a large clump of thick, impenetrable-looking trees and bushes.

Raoul slowed. 'Are you tired?'

'No, not at all.' In fact, she felt exhausted, but wanted desperately to prolong this moment, the nearest that Raoul had come to lowering his guard to her since their marriage.

He turned the horse in the direction of the ridge. 'Come, then. There is something that will interest you, I think.'

At the summit, he tied the bridle to a low-hanging branch, then, taking her by the hand, led her round the dense mass of hawthorn and elder, until he came to the place he was seeking, a large elder bush, covered with pale blossoms. He pulled some of the branches aside and motioned her past him. Puzzled, Jenni pushed her way in, brushing past the cloying sweetness of the elderflowers, then, as she broke through, she gasped in utter amazement. Whatever she might have expected, it was not this.

In front of her, in a small clearing, was a circle of gigantic granite stones, some still standing, thrusting up towards the purple-tinged sky, others lying shattered on the ground. In the pale, lambent light from the full midsummer moon which had just slid up into the sky, black, bottomless pools of shadow lay behind every stone. A sombre, brooding atmosphere hung over that hidden, enclosed place, and the fine hairs prickled suddenly on her neck, for she sensed instinctively that *something* was here—not in the least evil, but so old that it had become timeless.

Raoul was very close behind her. Through the cotton lawn of her blouse she could feel the warmth of his body, but she could not turn.

'Well, what do you think of it?'

'What is it?'

They were both, she realised, almost whispering, as though they were in some great cathedral.

'The archaeologists tell me that it is an outlier from the great Bronze Age stone rows at Carnac; it is not far as the crow flies. There are many stories attached to this place. The villagers, of course, insist that it is where the Druids performed their rites. They call it the Secret Grove. Others say that in this secluded bower, far from prying eyes, your Queen Guinevere met her lover, Lancelot.'

He put his hand on her arm and slowly drew her round to face him.

'Jenni?'

'Y—yes?'

She was trembling slightly now, and not from fear of this magical place. Somehow, though, she made herself look up at him. The moonlight had subtly altered his face, softening the hard lines of his mouth, while his eyes were silvery grey. She half closed hers against the expression in them and, hardly aware of what she was doing, put up her hand and very gently touched his cheek.

The next instant, Raoul had pulled her roughly to him and was smothering her face, her throat, with burning kisses, while his hand came up, taking possession of her breast. As she leaned towards him, his fingers closed on her blouse; he wrenched the buttons open and pulled it from her shoulders, exposing the pale skin of her breasts, first to his hands, then his mouth, until a shuddering gasp of pleasure was torn from her.

Her head was reeling dizzily and her last coherent thought was that this was totally different from that other time. Then, Raoul's lovemaking had been something gentle, unhurried, controlled, almost to the very end, but now she sensed the turbulent passion in him, while the scalding heat from his body was setting her alight too with a raging desire that he alone could quench.

He sank to his knees in front of her on the soft, mossy turf, his hands at the waistband of her skirt, and blindly she pressed his dark head to her stomach. Then she too slipped to her knees, her hands fumbling at the buttons of his white shirt, to move inside across the smooth skin, now damp

with perspiration. Raoul tore her skirt and flimsy briefs
from her, then moved away momentarily to drag off his
leather riding boots and trousers, before turning back to
her, his eyes dark with unconcealed passion.

Even so, she knew, he would still have been gentle with
her, but, consumed by a rapturous fire, she pulled him to
her. Their searching hands roved feverishly over each
other's body, awakening deep inside her undreamed-of
feelings of sensual ecstasy, until at last he groaned and
rolled over, pinning her beneath him. She arched to meet
him, in a splintering climax which sent the moon
plummeting drunkenly across the sky, and then, Raoul's
head on her breast, they both lay, lost in a languorous fulfil-
ment at the foot of the stones, which stood, silent witnesses
to their passion . . .

At last, after a long while, Raoul raised his head and
smiled at her, a smile that made her breath catch in her
throat. He drew back from her, then pulled her gently
upright against his damp body and softly kissed the side of
her throat.

'You must get dressed,' he whispered, and when she
murmured in sleepy protest he put a finger on her lips.
'Yes. The dew is falling. You will be ill, and anyway, my
wanton little wife,' he held her back from him and smiled at
her again, so that she was grateful for the night to hide her
blush, 'unlike poor Guinevere and Lancelot, we do have a
bedroom to return to.'

They rode back together in a hazy enchantment, Jenni
perched across his saddle, held safely in his arms, so that
she, unable ever to have enough of touching him, could give
him little nipping kisses on his throat and through his shirt,
until he threatened to stop and teach her a lesson then and
there.

It was the early hours when they let themselves into their apartment. Raoul insisted on her having a hot shower to take away the chill, so they showered together, she clinging to him, then he enfolded her in a bath towel and lifted her up into the wide bed . . .

She woke, to see him, fully dressed, bending over her, and for a moment she tensed, as her sleep-drugged brain re-enacted the scene of the morning after their wedding. But this time he took her hand and gently kissed the palm.

'So you are awake at last, my Sleeping Beauty.'

Jenni smiled up at him, lazily voluptuous, and his fingers tightened their grip.

'Do not look at me like that, *chérie*, or I shall find it impossible, not merely difficult, to leave you—and I must.'

'And suppose I tell you I don't want you to go, that I want you to stay with me?'

She gave a provocative pout, but Raoul silenced her with a gentle hand across her lips.

'I have to go, Jenni.' For a moment his face took on a serious, almost stern aspect. 'And no,' he went on firmly, as she tried to protest, 'you cannot come with me. It is purely business, you would be extremely bored, and anyway, I shall return tomorrow evening. But I swear,' he gave her a smile which made her pulses race, 'that very soon I shall take you away for that honeymoon I promised you.' And she had to content herself with that.

The long day dragged on but, although Jenni felt quite bereft without Raoul, the aching desolation of the previous days had vanished. Now she hungered for his return, a hunger which drove her by early evening to wander about the apartment, absently picking up ornaments and trailing a finger along the leather spines of books on the shelves. But at least the rooms were no longer haunted by Hélène Marquand, whose brooding presence, Jenni knew, had been purged for ever by the shared ecstasy of their lovemaking.

When, in the early evening, the phone rang, she almost ran to snatch up the receiver.

'Are you missing me?'

She closed her eyes against the sweet pleasure of hearing Raoul's deep voice. 'Where are you?'

'In a hotel in Bordeaux.'

'Are you alone?'

'No, I have François with me.'

François David, the lawyer? 'Is anything wrong?'

'No, nothing at all.' His voice was soothing. 'At least, nothing that need concern you, *ma petite.*'

But I do want to be concerned, she wanted to say, but Raoul interjected, his voice urgent, 'Jenni, I must go. The visitor we are expecting has arrived. *A demain, chérie.*' There was a click, then silence, and she slowly replaced the receiver.

The phone call, tantalisingly brief, had not brought her the reassurance of Raoul's presence, rather it had established the hundreds of miles between them, so now she took up her restless wandering once more, ending up in the office, where somehow she felt a little closer to him.

She sat in his leather chair, tipped out his neatly stacked pens and pencils and carefully rearranged them. There was a pile of papers and she began shuffling idly through them; then her eyes fell on the telephone answering machine. Perhaps she should check that there were no important messages, although what was the point when she could not contact Raoul? She tapped her fingers thoughtfully on the desk, then reached over and clicked down the switch.

There were several brief calls, including one in the

familiar tones of Claudette. Jenni smiled warmly to herself, then, as another voice began to speak, her fingers closed convulsively round the papers in front of her, crumpling them, as her face went blank with shock. This voice, too, was quite familiar, although she had heard that soft, husky timbre only once before, in a crowded street . . .

The tape ended. With a jerky, uncoordinated movement Jenni switched off the machine and sat staring at it, her face contorted as though from physical pain, until with a start she registered that Madame Cherbay was standing in the doorway.

'Shall I serve——' then, as Jenni stared at her with dazed, unseeing eyes, '—oh, *madame*, what is wrong? Are you ill?'

Somehow, she thought numbly, she had to pull herself together. Very slowly, leaning on the desk for support, she got to her feet.

'No, I'm all right.' She tried to assemble a reassuring smile on her face, although not only her features but her whole body seemed all at once to belong to someone else. 'I'm fine, really. I—I have a slight headache, that's all.'

It almost seemed too much effort to speak, and besides she was terribly afraid that at the very real concern in the housekeeper's voice she might break down, so she walked stiffly past her, like some mechanical doll that a child had set casually moving, and went through into the dining-room.

At dinner she ate almost nothing, but *Madame,* her eyes on Jenni's pale, set face, made no further comment, contenting herself with an occasional expressive click of the tongue. She had loaded the tray with untouched dishes and was opening the door when Jenni, driven by an impulse that she simply could not control, blurted out, '*Madame*——'

The word came out much louder than she had intended and the housekeeper looked round in surprise. 'I—I was just wondering,' under the shelter of the tablecloth, her fingers were closing and unclosing on each other, 'that is, will you tell me, please, where Madame Marquand lives?'

The woman gave one involuntary start, so that Jenni distinctly heard the crockery rattle faintly on the tray. She hesitated, almost as though to protest, Jenni thought, watching her closely. Like everyone else at Les Forêts, she obviously knew.

But then Madame Cherbay said, with slow reluctance, 'Yes, *madame*, she has that lodge-keeper's cottage at the far end of the estate.' She paused, then added, as though by inspiration, 'But I am sure that she is not there at present.'

Oh, but *madame*, you are wrong, Jenni thought savagely. At this very moment, she *is* there.

CHAPTER TWELVE

JENNI managed a brief, bright smile. 'Thank you. That will
be all.'

When the door had closed, she sat staring down at the
white linen cloth, picking abstractedly at its embroidered
edge with her nails. Hélène . . . actually on the estate, in
that pretty cottage. She heard her own voice, 'Does anyone
live there now?' and Raoul's guarded response, 'Oh, off and
on—mainly off.' She had sensed at the time that there was
some nuance, something which lay behind his careful reply.

And then another thought struck her, which came like a
physical blow in the pit of her stomach, so that she clapped
her hand to her mouth, almost retching. The cottage must
have been loaned to her by the lord of the manor—for
satisfactory services rendered, no doubt. Perhaps—she gave
a shudder of distaste—perhaps it had even been a touch of
droit de seigneur. Raoul had *enjoyed* Hélène—that was the
word, wasn't it?—before handing her over to a complaisant
husband, and now that he was married too, well, the cottage
would be even more convenient, a little love-nest for two.

Angry humiliation and jealousy surged through her like a
blood-red tide, so that she could have beaten her clenched
fists against the table. Then the tide ebbed, leaving her
instead shivering uncontrollably with shock. She chewed on
her lip, until she bit through the soft skin. What should she
do? What *could* she do? Gradually, very gradually, her mind
cleared, until it was icy clear.

She would—she *must* fight Hélène. She was Raoul's wife,

wasn't she? He had chosen to marry her. And after last
night—in spite of her angry misery, her face glowed at the
memory—surely she could win. She set her soft mouth in an
uncompromising line. Yes—she would win. Even now,
Hélène was awaiting Raoul. Well, she herself would keep
the rendezvous instead, and confront her. That was it—that
was what she must do, even though the very idea revolted
her.

Having made up her mind, she felt considerably better.
She went through to the bedroom, took off the simple
blouse and skirt that she was wearing and instead put on
one of the new dresses which Raoul had bought her, a slim-
fitting, deceptively simple shift in coarse, dark green linen.
She rearranged her hair in a smooth coil on her neck and
made up as carefully, she thought with a flash of her old
irony, as a Sioux brave on the eve of the most important
battle of his life.

She slipped out of a side door, and took a wildly
circuitous route, terrified that someone should see her and
guess where she was going. Once on the narrow gravelled
path, though, she was masked from any prying eyes by a
screen of shrubbery.

The door opened almost as she knocked, and in that stark
second, at her first real sight of Hélène Marquand, all
Jenni's carefully nurtured confidence melted away in one
violent lurch of despair. She was quite beautiful, with a sort
of stunning, utterly flawless beauty that could make a room
full of attractive, even lovely women appear—ordinary.
Thick, glossy blonde hair, huge, brilliant violet eyes, a full,
soft mouth, with only the faintest hint of petulance about it,
a slim yet voluptuously rounded figure.

She stared at Jenni for a moment, as though astonished,
then seemed to pull herself together.

'Why, what a charming surprise, Madame Kerouac.'

At least she made no pretence at not knowing her visitor's identity, Jenni thought with weary relief. But she should never have come here to face this woman. Too late, she knew it now.

Hélène hesitated, then opened the door a little wider.

'Please come in.' Her voice, though still husky, had lost a tiny part of its seductiveness, Jenni realised. No doubt its charm was not to be squandered lightly.

The small but luxuriously furnished sitting-room was the exact antithesis of everything in Raoul's apartment, Jenni registered with a swift yet comprehensive glance. Here, everything was soft and feminine: Hélène's heady, exotic perfume, the dainty pieces of light wood furniture, the Redouté flower prints on one wall, the pretty pink velvet *chaise-longue* and matching chairs, the huge sheepskin rug which covered half the dusky-pink carpet.

Hélène gestured Jenni to a chair and coiled herself gracefully on the *chaise-longue*, smoothing out the folds of her turquoise silk suit. She lit a cigarette from a slim gold lighter, not offering Jenni one, and through the haze of blue smoke gave her a long and finally openly dismissive look, so that Jenni had to clench her hands in her lap against the sludge of despairing defeat that was oozing into her body through every pore. How could she, totally inexperienced young girl that she was, ever have naïvely thought that she could take on and beat Hélène, who must surely be one of the most beautiful women in France? Even so, here, if ever, beauty was skin-deep. Jenni knew by unerring instinct that there was no goodness, no compassion behind the lovely mask.

Hélène smiled gently at her. 'You must forgive me, *madame,* for being perhaps less welcoming than I should have been. But I was expecting—someone else, and so——'

'I know who you were expecting,' Jenni said quietly, 'but, you see, my husband has been called away urgently, so I took your message.'

'Oh, heavens, how unfortunate.' Hélène gave a rueful, half-apologetic laugh. 'I am so sorry. You really must forgive me. Raoul would be so angry with me if he knew.'

More than anything Jenni wanted to leap to her feet, run away and hide herself, but somehow a terrible chill pride came to her rescue. Somehow, even now, she must endeavour to defeat this woman, or she herself would be destroyed. There would be no half measures.

'Please don't worry—about the phone call, that is,' she said. 'I know my husband is very anxious for me to get to know all our tenants on the estate, so it seemed appropriate for me to keep the appointment in his place.'

The other woman gave an angry intake of breath and ground out the cigarette in an astray. 'I really must disabuse you, Madame Kerouac, but I am not your tenant. You may have some tenuous claim to the rest of the estate—this cottage is mine.'

'But—but that's impossible!' Jenni stared at her, the exclamation torn from her. Raoul, so fiercely possessive of the Kerouac inheritance, would never have given away part of the estate. It was quite impossible, it had to be, for if not it could only mean that the unthinkable was true—that he loved Hélène, truly loved her, and not with any mere passing infatuation. It simply could not be true.

'I don't believe you,' she said finally.

Hélène shrugged carelessly, then, leaning across to the small side table, on which stood the telephone, lifted off the receiver with one slender finger and held it out towards Jenni.

'If you wish to establish the truth, please ring François David——

'No, *madame*.' Jenni shook her head, trying to free herself from a numbing listlessness that was creeping stealthily over her. 'It doesn't matter.'

The other woman was watching her shrewdly. 'It has been rather a shock for you. I begged Raoul to inform you. I told him that you would almost certainly hear gossip, but for whatever reason, he did not wish to.'

'But he has told me,' Jenni responded, somehow injecting a faint trace of her old spirit into her voice. 'He also told me that the affair is long over between you.'

Hélène gave another elegant shrug, which subtly managed to convey silent insolence. 'If that is what he chose to tell you, that is his business. Of course,' she continued, her voice softly reminiscent, as though she were reliving past scenes, 'we have known one another for many years. When Raoul was younger, it was so easy to hold him in the palm of my hand,' she curved her silver-tipped fingers in a vivid gesture of possession, which intensified Jenni's feelings of malaise into a spasm of real nausea, 'and I can keep him here still for as long as I wish.'

So it really was true. The affair had not ended. Goaded beyond bearing, Jenni sprang to her feet, staring down at Hélène.

'Yes, but he didn't marry you, did he? He could have done, but he married me.'

Hélène looked up at her in mild amazement. 'But my dear child, how could he?'

Caught off balance for a moment, Jenni frowned at her. 'You mean, your marriage? Well, you could surely have got a divorce.'

'Oh, heavens, yes! A divorce would have been very

simple. My husband and I have led separate existences for many years——' something, the merest flicker of—was it bitterness, or at least regret?—had entered her voice, and Jenni had a fleeting vision of a withered, sterile marriage, so that her heart was wrung for an instant with pity, but then Hélène's former flint-like hardness reasserted itself '—I would never presume to question him about his conduct, and he, in turn, is fully understanding of my private life. An entirely civilised arrangement which, I assure you, is quite customary.'

Yet again, Jenni felt that she had betrayed herself as a prim, unworldly English innocent, behaving somehow in a totally unreasonable way. What was that old story, about Frenchmen setting the expense of their mistresses, like business lunches, against their tax bills? It was surely a myth, yet it said something for the blasé manner in which such relationships were seemingly regarded. And yet surely Raoul——

'But there was no need for a divorce.' Hélène's remorseless voice was pressing on. 'Our relationship—Raoul's and mine—has always been perfectly satisfactory, in every way.' She gave Jenni a swift, telling look. 'But then, once the terms of your grandmother's will became known, and you appeared—well, he had no choice. He had to marry you.'

Had to marry? So her own fears had, after all, been correct all along. Jenni forced herself to meet Hélène's eyes, which flickered over her with a contempt which was now quite undisguised.

'But of course it will not last. Only until you give him that child he needs so badly. And once the entire estate is in Raoul's hands, how long do you imagine he will keep you, a young, immature girl, a nobody?'

She shot Jenni a slanting look, then laughed. 'Oh, my

poor child! Raoul has obviously been very remiss. He has
clearly omitted to reveal to you the main terms of the will.'

Jenni sat down suddenly. A cold finger of panic touched
her spine, and the ground seemed almost to move under her
feet, as though from an impending avalanche. She
moistened her dry lips.

'Reveal what?'

'Why, that when you have a child, you lose everything.
Your share of the estate passes immediately to that child,
under the direct control, not of you, but of Raoul. And you
surely do not imagine that he will then want anything more
from you?'

Of course. That look which had flashed from Raoul to
François David, that unspoken warning. The avalanche was
upon her, carrying her away, and she leaped to her feet,
blundering out into the hall. Hélène followed her and
paused, a hand on the doorknob as Jenni stood, her face
averted.

'Please, I beg you, do not tell Raoul of my error over the
telephone. He would be so very angry with me.'

'Do not alarm yourself, *madame*, I shall not tell him.'
Jenni spoke through tight lips. Another few moments and
she was quite certain that she would be physically sick all
over this soft cream carpet.

'Are you quite well?' Hélène asked solicitously. 'I am
sorry. Your grandmother did not perhaps anticipate such a
consequence. Of course,' she smiled conspiratorially, 'the
solution might be for you to ensure that you do not become
pregnant—although that, of course, would be to deprive
Raoul of the child he so desires. But if you and I were
superstitious,' she gave a light laugh, which plucked at
Jenni's overstretched nerves, 'which of course we are not, I
would advise you not to allow Raoul to take you to the place

the local people call the Secret Grove.' Jenni's eyes, wide
with startled apprehension, flew momentarily to her face,
then slid away again as Hélène paused for effect, before
adding, 'For years, village couples have gone there when
they have failed to conceive comfortably at home in bed.
They consider its influence to be—infallible.'

Somehow, Jenni got herself back to the château and the
privacy of the apartment unseen. Dry-eyed, she stripped off
her clothes, showered and lay down, staring at the ceiling.
    The night seemed endless, but finally she dropped off
into a restless, tormented sleep, only to rouse again at dawn,
violently ill. Afterwards, she huddled on the cold floor of
the bathroom, leaning her head against the tiled wall and
wiping the drops of perspiration from her forehead with
clammy fingers. Nevertheless, it did seem, after she had
forced herself to shower and dress, as if something of the
polluting poison of Hélène had drained from her system
along with the sickness.
    Even so, as she mechanically ate the croissants Madame
Cherbay had brought her for breakfast, she had to force
herself to think back over the previous evening's events, for
her whole body, and also her mind, still felt raw from the
encounter.
    Just how much truth had there been in Hélène's words?
She had surely been right about the will—she would not
have lied over something so easily verified. Jenni raised her
eyes from her plate to the portrait on the wall opposite her,
then raised her cup in a bitter, ironic salute. 'Game, set and
match to you, Grand-mère.'
    But then her lips tightened. So the old lady had not really
repented, after all, as Jenni had so fondly imagined,
wistfully believing that if only she had appeared on the

scene before her grandmother's death she would have been welcomed, even loved. But no, she was merely to be used to provide a Kerouac heir for the Kerouac inheritance.

Was Hélène also right, though, in her taunt that Jenni would be discarded as soon as a child was born? Surely Raoul could not be so cruel? Hélène was clearly a totally self-absorbed, vindictive woman who had taken a malicious delight in Jenni's distress, and perhaps, in spite of Hélène's warning, a child would in fact bind her and Raoul more tightly. On the other hand, he had never made any secret of his determination to retain sole control over Les Forêts . . .

As for Hélène's parting shot about the Secret Grove—she could surely never have realised how that barb would strike home. Nevertheless, Raoul would not believe such a ridiculous old wives' tale; whatever else he might be, he was not a superstitious peasant . . .

And what, finally—Jenni forced herself to confront this, the most crucial question of all—of Hélène's boast that the affair was still alive? There was just one thread of tenuous hope, and Jenni clung to this. Hélène was unaware of their lovemaking, sensual and passionate, at the Grove, then at the château; could not have guessed at the shared ecstasy that Raoul had guided them to. And yet there was, inescapably, that message on the answering machine so confidently making the assignation . . . Perhaps, after all, Raoul was perfectly capable of running two close relationships in tandem . . .

Jenni pressed her hands to her head, trying vainly to clear the muddled thoughts that were tumbling pell-mell through her mind. How she needed the reassurance of Raoul's presence! If only she could hear his firm tread along the passage outside. Desperately, she willed him to appear in the doorway, but only the maid came in, to clear away the remains of her breakfast. Raoul would not return until evening.

She simply could not bear another solitary day moping around the house and grounds, afraid now that the estate staff all knew, if not everything, a great deal. She would lose herself in the anonymity of the market town a few miles away . . .

But even here, the same restlessness pursued her, so that she wandered around quite aimlessly. It was market day, and she found herself eventually in the square, drifting past pens of sad-eyed cattle and almost oblivious of the curious glances she was attracting. It was very hot—too hot, the sun burning against her bare head and shoulders.

Just round the corner, she knew, there was a small café, full of farmers and market workers, no doubt, but at least she would be able to get an iced drink there and sit in the shade for a while. Yes, that was what she would do, but first she really must lean against this pen of calves, because everything was all at once moving around her in a slow, yet disturbing minuet . . .

She was lying on a white couch, and bending towards her, out of the mist which was slowly clearing, was a face which she ought to know.

'Now, my dear Madame Kerouac, do not alarm yourself.'

The face smiled down at her reassuringly. Of course, it was old Doctor Cottard, who had come to Les Forêts a couple of times the week before, when Raoul's stable boy had fallen from the hay loft. But—*she* wasn't ill, was she? She tried to sit up, but then sank back, staring up at him, as a flicker of dizziness swept over her.

'I—I fainted, didn't I? I remember now—it was very hot.'

'Yes, that is right, *madame*. And as my surgery is just off the square, they brought you here, one of your husband's tenant farmers carrying you as tenderly as a kitten.'

Jenni sat up and gratefully sipped the glass of cold water he held for her. 'I'm sorry to have been such a trouble to you.' She smiled at him rather weakly, as he spread his hands self-deprecatingly. 'I've never fainted before, but it was so hot out there.'

She fumbled for her bag, hardly taking in the doctor's words, but then she sat very still, slowly nodding. 'Yes, I *was* sick this morning.'

Pregnant? 'But that's impossible!' she blurted out, then blushed scarlet as the doctor gave her a long look over his spectacles. 'I—I mean——' She stopped dead, biting her lip. With a lightning flash of certainty, she knew that he was right.

'Don't let him take you to the Sacred Grove . . .' But why not, when Raoul had already made love to her in that secluded barn? What a fool she had been, dismissing her long overdue period as a casualty of the stressed events of the past weeks.

She stared wildly at him, and he, mistaking her expression, put a fatherly hand on her arm.

'Don't be afraid, my dear. It is natural for young mothers—and you are very young—to be a little apprehensive, but we will take good care of you. As for that scoundrel, Raoul, he will be delighted, you will see.'

He smiled at her, inviting her to share his pleasure in her news. 'I told him only recently that it was time he settled down to be a family man, and it seems he has very quickly taken my advice.'

Jenni's face seemed to be made of cardboard, but somehow she returned his smile, and managed at last to escape.

Once inside her hot, airless van, she wanted nothing more than simply to lean her head down against the steering wheel, close her eyes and drift away, past thought, but she forced herself instead to fumble for her car keys and drive off.

'When you have a child, you lose everything . . .' Hélène's voice kept pace with the wheels, and Jenni winced, then hastily corrected the steering as a warning blast jerked her back to the present reality. She drove on more slowly, certain all at once of only one thing: that events now had taken control of her, as though she were no more than a puppet, and were speeding her along helplessly to some inevitable conclusion—but what?

She bit back a small, unhappy sob. She wanted desperately to bear Raoul's child, feel the first faint flutterings of his baby under her heart, and yet, perhaps, for her this birth might bring only desolation and sorrow, if she really were to be set aside, discarded, as Hélène had so triumphantly claimed. After all, Raoul had never actually told her that he loved her, only called her *'ma petite'*, and made love to her, which was not at all the same thing.

Discarded. The word was still tolling like a knell in her ears as she turned into the drive. She had left earlier by the front entrance and now, too late, she realised, with an unpleasant, sinking sensation, that unthinkingly she had returned by the road which passed Hélène's cottage. For a moment her foot hovered above the brake. It was not too late to reverse and go the long way round, but surely there was no point. Hélène would hardly be lying in wait for her among the bushes—she smiled momentarily at this incongruous picture—and anyway she need not look, only keep her gaze undeviatingly on the road ahead.

She was almost past when, as though endowed with a will

of their own, her eyes strayed. She took one horrified look, then accelerated away fast round the bend, to pull up sharply just out of sight, her hands shaking, as if with fever, so that she could hardly switch off the engine.

Perhaps, after all, it had not been Raoul's car. There were plenty of silver-grey Citroëns in Brittany. Oh, come on, you fool, she castigated herself savagely, losing your mind now, as well as everything else, are you? Don't pretend. You saw him, didn't you? You saw him, with Hélène, her arm round him, *pawing* him, leading him into her cottage.

So Hélène had spoken the truth, after all. What she had tried to convince herself were the corrosive lies of a vindictive woman were nothing more than the simple truth. She was right about the affair—she was surely also right about the child.

Just for a moment, the bleak vision of the empty, loveless years ahead washed through Jenni, then faded, leaving her, she was positive, thinking with crystal clarity for the first time in weeks, certainly since the first fatal meeting with that grey-eyed stranger in the lane. All unknowing, she had lost Raoul on that distant morning in the barn—though how could you lose something you had never really had? Her eyes filled with tears but, furious at her weakness, she blinked them away.

Unbidden, the line of the song from that morning in her grandmother's bedroom came hauntingly to her. For the next few months she would indeed be only a bird in a gilded cage. 'We will take good care of you . . . Raoul will be delighted . . .' Of course he would—that poor, innocent doctor could have no conception—she giggled for a moment at the cleverness of her own pun—of just how delighted Raoul would be.

Raoul. Just for a moment, she let herself see him as he

had been—hardly hours before, she realised with surprise, though it now seemed like months, even years. But then she forced his image from her. She was going to leave him, and she would never be able to do that if she weakly allowed herself to keep the memory of his eyes, his mouth . . .

Leave him? Of course—the thought had leaped uncalled into her mind, but now, with this new clarity, she could see that this was the only thing to do. But Raoul had once threatened to hunt her down—and now he would have even greater cause. So she must hide herself very securely from him . . .

Feeling almost light-headed, she let herself silently into the château, seen by no one. She tiptoed, breath suspended, down the passage to the sitting-room, then thought, this is ridiculous. I'm like an intruder in my own home. But of course this was not her home, and never would be now.

She found the number she wanted, lifted the receiver very carefully, and dialled.

'You are fortunate, *madame*. There is a cancellation for vehicle and passenger on the ferry leaving Roscoff at ten tonight. And the name?'

She did not hesitate.

'Jenni Green.'

CHAPTER THIRTEEN

SHE threw a few things into her old weekend bag, leaving almost everything that Raoul had given her, then checked that she had enough money for the ferry. She was almost out of the apartment when she remembered her passport. After a silent, frenzied search, she found it at last in the office filing cabinet, intended to be safely under lock and key, no doubt. She straightened up slowly and opened it. Goodbye, Eugénie Kerouac—not that you've ever really existed, have you? Welcome back, Jenni Green.

She hesitated a moment then, almost unwillingly, pulled Raoul's memo pad towards her, scribbled a couple of lines and left it on the desk, half out of sight behind some papers, As she went out, she heard footsteps and voices, and she froze, her heart thumping erratically, but the sounds went on past the door.

A few moments later, she scrambled into the van. For a second, she felt almost grateful to Raoul for insisting that René spray it a refined *bleu-marine;* unlike pink dolphins, a discreet navy would give her the anonymity she needed on the road, for Raoul, she knew, would soon be hunting for her. He needed her—or rather, he needed their child.

But even so, she must hurry, she thought in sudden terror, for he might arrive at any instant. At the thought, a bitter, choking sensation filled her throat. Raoul would be occupied for several hours; no doubt he had contacted Hélène and arranged his early return, while telling *her* that he would be back that evening . . .

* * *

Careless of whether she lived or died, Jenni saw nothing of
that long journey, yet some providence brought her
unscathed to join the snaking queue of cars beneath the
white, looming shape of the ferry. She tapped her fingers on
the wheel, afraid lest even at this moment Raoul should
somehow appear in front of her, dark and threatening, so
that when she was at last beckoned on, the van leaped
forward under her eager hands.

By the time she wandered out on to the deck, it was
almost dark and she found herself alone. She leaned over
the rail, watching as the final few lorries, bulging with
cauliflowers, manoeuvred slowly down the ramp, where
orange-overalled men were already at work uncoiling the
massive ropes.

So had she leaned, almost on this spot, on that far-off
morning and seen that silver-grey Citroën sweep down and
stop beneath her. Hélène—she who had been the hidden
motif throughout their relationship, and now had won—and
Raoul. The knife twisted in her heart again, and she
squeezed her eyes tight shut, as a tear oozed slowly out. Oh,
God, she loved him. How could she ever live without seeing
him once more?

Her eyes flew wide open. She couldn't. She had to see
him again. Perhaps, eventually, it would be easier for her to
tear herself from him, but now—now, she wanted him,
needed him, and the need was tearing her apart inside.

She flew down one iron staircase after another, thrusting
people heedlessly aside in her frantic haste. In the hold,
thick with sickening exhaust fumes, she caught hold
beseechingly of a man's arm, shouting to make herself
heard, gesticulating wildly in the direction of her van, but
he only shook his head with a negative finality that chilled
her.

She swung round. The ramp was already, almost imperceptibly, inching up. She did not allow herself to hesitate. Ignoring the shouts behind her, and a man who advanced on her, his arms waving, his mouth frozen open with shock, she scrambled up the ramp, then flung herself across the narrow gap of oily water which had appeared between the ramp edge and the sloping concrete jetty.

She landed on all fours, grazing her hands, though she was hardly aware of the smarting pain. Standing up shakily, she forced herself up the deserted jetty. Behind her, the ramp clanked into place, there was a blast from the funnel, and when she turned the ferry was already gliding away, its lights reflecting in the strip of water which was widening with every moment.

Only then did Jenni finally awaken to what she had done. She had no car and—she registered the fact now, though without interest—she had left her bag, with her money and passport, on the deck. This time she had mugged herself, she thought, and choked down the slightly hysterical laugh which welled up.

There was no one around, and it was dark anyway, now. But still she felt nervously conspicuous. Near the jetty was a wall of huge piled-up chunks of rock and concrete, a rough breakwater against winter storms. She walked over to it and huddled between two rocks, glad of their shelter, for it had begun to drizzle.

At the far end of the jetty were rows of fluorescent lights, their reflections glimmering on the rain-soaked tarmac. Already far out to sea, the ferry was a ghostly outline. Jenni was utterly alone. She leaned her head back, but there was no comfort in the rough granite.

A car sped down the hill and on to the quay. It stopped, its wheels barely a foot from the edge; a man got out and stood rigid, staring after the ferry.

Raoul? But it couldn't be. Raoul was still at Les Forêts.
She must be suffering from delusions, her despairing need
for him conjuring him up from nowhere. As Jenni walked
towards him, her hands outstretched to him, the man
banged his fist down on the car roof in a gesture of impotent
frustration, then froze motionless as he caught sight of her.

His face was sombre under the lights, his eyes and mouth
thrown into deep shadow, so that all at once he did indeed
seem a stranger, remote, perhaps even dangerous. Her
hands dropped limply to her sides, but she willed herself
somehow to keep walking forward, although he did not
move a muscle, only watched her intently. They regarded
each other in silence for a few moments.

'So, despite your best efforts, you were too late.' His voice
held an odd, strained note and his eyes flickered past her.
'But where is your van?'

'Oh, out there.' Jenni pointed in the vague direction of
the sea.

Raoul raised his brows questioningly, and she added, 'On
the ferry, with my bag.'

'Oh.'

'H—how——' the word came out as a husky croak, so she
cleared her throat '—how did you know where I'd gone? I'm
sure I didn't say in the note.'

A fleeting spasm crossed his face, but when he spoke his
voice was under tight control. ' "Dear Raoul, please forgive
me, I'm sorry, Jenni." No, you did not say. But other
people can use the telephone, you know. No Madame
Kerouac was booked on the ferry, so on a faint hope I tried
Jenni Green.'

He stopped abruptly for a moment, then, as though his
iron control had snapped, he burst out, 'Oh, *mon dieu,* how

could you do it to me, Jenni? Can you not guess what I have been through since I got back to Les Forêts?' He ran his fingers through his hair. 'I did not even realise that you were gone until Cottard rang me to ask how you were. He had been extremely concerned by your reaction when he told you that he was almost certain that you were expecting a baby.'

'Oh, yes, of course—the baby,' Jenni said dully.

Raoul gave an incoherent exclamation, then, the next moment, he had snatched her to him so tightly that she could hardly draw breath.

'Don't look like that, Jenni, I beg you.' He began to rock her in his arms, his chin against her soft hair. 'He thought you were frightened. I feel very badly—you are so young.' He seemed almost to be speaking to himself, his voice rough, as he tilted her face gently towards him and gave her a ragged smile. 'Forgive me, *ma petite*. It was just that, that morning——'

Jenni shivered suddenly and he broke off. He took hold of one of her hands and gave a smothered exclamation. 'You are frozen.'

He opened the car door and bundled her in, then flung himself in beside her. He switched on the interior light and for a long moment they stared at one another. In the subdued light, Raoul looked pale and drawn; his hair was untidy, there were dark shadows under his eyes, and his mouth was a harsh line.

Shakily, she said, 'You need a shave. You look awful.'

'So do you.'

His smile was tight, but she sensed him relax a fraction. He took her cold hands and began chafing them in his warm ones.

'I can understand you being frightened, but you should

not have run away from me.'

'I know. I'm sorry,' she said softly. 'I must have been crazy, I think, but you see, once I knew—about the will, I mean, from Hélène—I thought you wouldn't w-want me, after the baby was born, and I couldn't bear it.'

Raoul swore savagely under his breath. 'But Jenni, you must surely have realised that Hélène is an angry, disappointed woman. Why did you choose to believe her?'

'But the cottage. She said you gave it to her, so I thought——' She broke off, biting her lip.

'You thought it was our private—love-nest.' He gave a long sigh. 'Jenni, your grandmother gave Hélène the cottage. I did not want to tell you—I thought it would disturb you.' His lips tightened in anger. 'I have tried to keep too much from you. If I had told you, perhaps you would have been less ready to lap up her poison.'

Very gently, he began stroking his thumb across the back of her hand. 'You see, your grandmother and Hélène's mother were close friends. Although Hélène was much younger than your father, it was always understood that they would marry. But Philippe would have none of it; he broke free and married an English girl.' He shot Jenni a faint smile. 'Although Hélène was only a girl, her intense pride was badly damaged, and your grandmother left her the cottage—one small part of the Kerouac estate—as some sort of reparation. She never really loved me, I am sure, and once you—Philippe's child—had arrived, I think her main objective was somehow to wound you. And she has succeeded—I see the pain in your eyes still.'

'But this afternoon—I saw you going into her cottage, and——'

'And so, once again, you added two and two and made five.' He shook his head, half angry, half exasperated. 'I

think I have been too indulgent with you. I should have
shaken some sense into that beautiful head of yours long
ago.' He drew a deep breath, then went on, 'Leaving for
Bordeaux yesterday morning was one of the hardest things I
have ever done; I had physically to tear myself away. I went
only because of a catastrophe that could have ruined us.
You have, I think, sensed that I have been rather—
preoccupied, over the past few weeks.'

He smiled grimly, as Jenni stared at him, wide-eyed. 'It
was an added burden to try to shield you from the
knowledge that we have been threatened with law suits that
could have brought down the whole Kerouac estate. Oh,
yes, it was as bad as that. Our agent in Bordeaux, a man I
have known and trusted for ten years, has been busy
diluting our top quality wine with an inferior *vin de table*
and distributing it under our label.

'We have been discreetly investigating him for some time,
but it was only two nights ago that I received the telephone
call confirming that we had the evidence we needed. We
confronted him, François and I, and he has now been
thrown to the wolves,' he looked at her, chill-eyed, 'and the
estate has avoided a terrible scandal. I left François to sort
out the details and set out at once for home—much to his
ribald amusement.'

'But you didn't come straight home.' Jenni could not
quite keep the note of accusation from her voice.

'No. If only I had—but on the long drive back I had time
for some hard thinking, and I finally realised the folly of
permitting Hélène to remain on the estate, if only for the
brief periods when she was not in Paris—I had not forgotten
how you reacted to seeing her before the wedding, although
I did not realise then just how dangerous she could be. So I
stopped at the cottage to make her an offer to purchase it,

at a price that she would find hard to refuse. But there was
no need. She informed me that she was leaving anyway, that
she was moving out straight away. I did not realise why she
was suddenly so accommodating—until later.' His face was
grim.

'When I got back to the château and Cottard rang——' his
hands closed convulsively on hers for an instant '—it was
then that Madame Cherbay broke down in hysterics and
told me—between shrieks,' he added drily, 'that you had
been enquiring about Hélène.'

'Oh,' said Jenni breathlessly, feeling a sudden twinge of
horrified sympathy for Hélène. 'What did you do?'

'I went back and threatened—yes,' there was the barest
glimmer of a smile, 'I did threaten her, and she told me
what she had done. I had seen her briefly at the filling
station in the village before setting out for Bordeaux, so she
knew that it was likely that you would play back the answering machine. She claims that it began as no more than a
foolish game, to get under your skin, but she realises now
that it got out of hand—especially her telling you about that
appalling clause in the will. But Jenni,' his voice was
suddenly very gentle, 'why did you choose to believe an
embittered woman, when everyone else knows the truth?'

'What do you mean?' She frowned at him blankly.

'Why, that I am crazy about you, of course.'

'You—love me?'

Raoul gave her a wry look. 'Well, that is one very
restrained way of expressing it. Some people would say that
I am totally besotted by you.' His smile was faintly rueful.
'No doubt I am the laughing-stock of the entire estate, from
François David downwards—the cool, aloof Raoul Kerouac
behaving like a feverish schoolboy. After our wedding
night, only my pride, the memory of what I had told you—

that I had never yet taken a woman by force—and,' he hesitated, 'yes—a certain guilt that I had taken advantage of your youth to rush you into a marriage that I began to fear you had been ill-prepared for, enabled me to put a rein on my own desires, my burning need to possess you again.'

He grimaced. 'My affair with Hélène continuing? The simple truth is I have not been able to look at another woman, much less make love to one, since the first day I met you, and she knew it.' He broke off abruptly to look searchingly at her. 'But you realised that, surely?'

'I—I didn't know what to think, but in the end I really did believe that you'd only married me for the estate, and then——'

'Oh, damn the estate to perdition!' He banged his fist impatiently down on the steering wheel. 'Since that first moment in the lane, you were a fever in my blood. I seized on Marie-Christine's indiscretion as the chance to keep you near me. I could hardly believe my good fortune when you agreed to work at the campsite, and then, when I was forced to go away, the journey home had never seemed so long. When I saw your passport and the letter, and realised who you were, I tried extremely hard to convince myself that you were a scheming, unscrupulous young woman—I think I succeeded for a while, but then, by the next morning, I knew that it was no use. Unscrupulous or not, my feelings for you had not changed . . . The car accident was heaven-sent. I magnified the damage, of course, hardly able to believe that I should have you to myself for a whole night. Nevertheless, I managed to keep my yearning for you under control during that night—even when you so kindly allowed me to have a half-share in your bed,' his smile had a heart-stopping tenderness, 'although I must confess that I had to resort to the trick of pretending to fall asleep, when sleep

was the furthest thought from my mind! But the next
morning, it was impossible—I could hold out no longer. All
the same,' his expression grew serious, 'I was greatly at
fault, to take advantage of your innocence. Can you ever
forgive me, *chérie?*'

There was a poignant, almost pleading note in his voice,
which went through her. She raised his hands to her lips
and very gently kissed them, then smiled up at him
tremulously.

'There's nothing to forgive. I love you and I'm having
your child. What more could I possibly want?'

Momentarily, she glimpsed the sheen of tears in his eyes,
then he gathered her to him wordlessly.

A long while later, he said into her hair, 'Jenni?'

'Mmmm.'

'Jenni, there is something you must do. I want you to
forgive Hélène.' He hesitated. 'I know that she has almost
succeeded in ruining both our lives, but she is a deeply
unhappy woman, and her shadow may hang over our
happiness if you do not. After all, you have won, and she
knows that.'

She stiffened in his arms. Forgive Hélène? The woman
who had striven so unscrupulously to drive them apart?
Whose gratuitous cruelty had cost her so much unhappiness? Never.

She drew back and looked up into the strained face
of—her husband. He was still wrong, of course, in one
thing. Hélène had loved him, and loved him still, with
quiet desperation. From somewhere very deep, beneath all
the anger, an overpowering compassion welled up inside
her. What had Raoul said? You have won. It was true—she
had Raoul and he loved her. She had to grow up. She
should be, not childishly vindictive, but magnanimous.

She smiled at him. 'Yes—I forgive her.'

'And you are quite happy about the baby?'

Dizzy with joy, she could only give him a radiant smile, but the shadow on his face cleared at last. Very gently, he drew her to him and kissed her.

'Oh, *ma petite,*' he said against her lips.

'No,' she said firmly. 'Not *ma petite.*'

He laughed softly. 'You are quite right. You are my wife—and my partner.'

'And you will let me help you, with running Les Forêts, I mean?'

'Of course I will,' Raoul smiled indulgently, 'in any way you wish. Except for one thing.' When she looked at him questioningly, he added, 'You will be far too occupied in the coming months for any nonsense about guided tours. So yes, I must no longer treat you as a child.' He gave her a look which set up a breathless, fluttery feeling inside her. 'Let me see. Would "my adored wife" please you a little more?'

She managed somehow to give him a mischievous grin. 'Mmmm. I dare say that will do to be going on with.'

Raoul dropped another light, cherishing kiss on her forehead. 'And that also will have to do to be going on with, as you so elegantly express it. For now, I must contact the ferry company about your bag—and I presume you will want that disreputable vehicle of yours to be returned? I can ring from a restaurant.' He scrutinised her sternly. 'Have you eaten today?'

'Well . . .' Jenni wrinkled her brow—it was so difficult to remember. 'Not since breakfast,' she admitted guiltily.

'Tch.' His expression was almost angry. 'It is high time someone took care of you. You are clearly incapable of looking after yourself. So, first a meal, and then I must get you to a hotel—you are exhausted.'

'Oh no, please, Raoul.' She hastily stifled a huge yawn. 'Please, not a hotel. Take me back to Les Forêts.'

He frowned at her. 'Another long, tiring journey, in your condition? Certainly not.'

Oh, my handsome, adorable, *bossy* husband, she thought suddenly. How you do like to have everything your own way! Well, we'll just have to see from now on, won't we?

'Please, Raoul,' she said, very softly, and put up a hand to caress his cheek . . .

As Raoul lifted her out of the car, Madame Cherbay hurried down the steps. 'Oh, *monsieur*, thank God you found her.' Her face was strained, and Jenni, infinitely touched by her concern, managed a tired smile of reassurance, before leaning her head against Raoul's comforting shoulder.

In the hall he paused and looked down at her. '*Madame* says do you want anything to eat? She has a meal ready.'

Jenni shook her head. 'No, I just want to go to bed.'

He set her down carefully on the edge of the bed and sat beside her. Very gently, as though she were an unresisting child, he undressed her, put on her nightdress and laid her back against the pillow.

'Just before you sleep, there is someone who is very anxious to meet you.'

He gave her a smile, went out and came back a few moments later with a large wicker hamper. He put it down on the bed beside her, opened it and, as Jenni gave a gasp of delighted surprise, lifted out a small creamy puppy. She hauled herself up on the pillow and Raoul dropped the struggling creature on to her lap.

'A late wedding present. If I had not stopped to collect

her, I would have been here in time——'

She saw that shadow in his eyes again and said quickly, 'You're so good to me. Thank you.'

'I thought that you were becoming dangerously fond of Igor—he is very old, you know. This,' he gestured a finger towards the heap of silky fur cradled in her arms, 'is Natasha, Igor's great-granddaughter.'

He scooped up the puppy and stood up. 'You shall see her again when you wake.'

When he came back, Jenni said anxiously, 'Is she all right?'

He grinned. 'I imagine so. I left her biting Igor's tail, while *Madame* was grinding up a disgusting mixture of steak and liver.'

He sat down and she leaned against him, her head on his chest.

'Thank you, Jenni.' His voice was a soft whisper.

'For what?' She too was whispering.

'For returning to me—for that leap off the ferry, though I should scold you for that—and for giving me our child.'

He slid one hand around her, to splay his fingers possessively across her flat stomach, and the expression in his eyes when she looked up at him made her breath catch painfully in her chest. A little bubble of joyful rapture slowly grew inside her, then popped, as though showering her with happiness.

She leaned her head against him again and very carefully began unbuttoning his shirt.

'No, what are you doing?' Raoul protested. 'You said you were tired.'

'No, I did not. I said I wanted to go to bed.' She gave him a deliberately provocative smile. 'And that's not the same thing at all, is it?'

'But, *ma petite*—I'm sorry—my beloved wife. You must rest.'

She shook her head at him. 'I rested all the way home. And you haven't answered my question. It isn't the same thing at all, is it?'

She took his hand and began gently, sensuously, drawing her tongue across the strong palm.

Raoul sighed dramatically. 'I can see that I have encumbered myself for life with a wayward, disobedient wife.'

Very softly, with his little finger, he lifted the silk strap of her nightdress away from her shoulder. He trailed his lips down the line of her neck and whispered against the erratic pulse at her throat, 'But you are quite right, *chérie*. It is not the same at all.'

Harlequin Superromance

Here are the longer, more involving stories you have been waiting for... Superromance.

Modern, believable novels of love, full of the complex joys and heartaches of real people.

Intriguing conflicts based on today's constantly changing life-styles.

Four new titles every month.
Available wherever paperbacks are sold.

SUPER-1